Nancy Lavo creates sweet, contemporary Christian fiction. She truly delivered A Slice of Paradise in the second book of the Lone Star Loves series. God speaks to us in various ways, including fiction with well-crafted, realistic characters like Mary Jo Piermont. A Slice of Paradise will make you smile, make you laugh out loud, and bring tears to your eyes.
—**Connie Lewis Leonard**, author of the In Texas contemporary Christian romance series

In this gift-of-a-second-chance story, Lavo beautifully depicts the power of love and kindness to change lives.
—**Lynne Gentry**, USA TODAY bestselling author

Nancy Lavo has done it again. A Slice of Paradise is a sweet concoction of deliciousness, a perfect rendition of the enemies-to-lovers story. The journey Eden and Joe take while their relationship develops is completely believable and will have you cheering them on. Chock full of interesting side characters, some we already know from Lavo's previous book, the pages abound with multiple opportunities to laugh. Like, out loud. Lavo's dialogue is spot-on and natural, giving the banter between Eden and Joe an authentic and humorous flair. And her description of the lovely house will draw pictures in your mind of wonderful Southern charm. When Lavo depicts how God can help a person forgive and accept the abundant life He wants to offer, you'll have tears in your eyes. Another blue ribbon creation for Lavo. Bravo!
—**Paula Peckham**, award-winning author of the San Antonio series

LONE STAR LOVES

A Slice of Paradise

BOOK 2

NANCY LAVO

Birmingham, Alabama

A Slice of Paradise
Iron Stream Fiction
An imprint of Iron Stream Media
100 Missionary Ridge
Birmingham, AL 35242
IronStreamMedia.com

This is a work of fiction. Names, characters, and incidents are all products of the author's imagination or are used for fictional purposes. Any mentioned brand names, places, and trademarks remain the property of their respective owners, bear no association with the author or the publisher, and are used for fictional purposes only.

Library of Congress Control Number: 2023932305

Cover design by For the Muse Designs
ISBN: 978-1-56309-639-6 (paperback)
ISBN: 978-1-56309-640-2 (e-book)
1 2 3 4 5—28 27 26 25 24

DEDICATION

This book is dedicated to my wonderful family.
Thank you, heavenly Father, for placing me in the
midst of such a loud and lovely group.

ACKNOWLEDGMENTS

So many people to thank!

My critique group is the best. It's a blessing to write and learn with this incredibly supportive group of women.

The team at Iron Stream Media is a delight to work with. I'm grateful for their patience and professionalism as we work to craft the best possible book. Many thanks to Larry J. Leech II, my editor extraordinaire, for your insight and attention to detail.

My agent, Tamela Hancock-Murray, is a fountain of knowledge and encouragement. I'm so glad to have her in my corner.

Finally, thanks to my husband and family for bringing such joy to my life.

CHAPTER ONE

Mary Jo Piermont awakened at precisely three o'clock a.m. for the fourth night in a row.

She's coming.

She scooted herself upright and spoke into the darkened room as she had the previous nights. "Yes, Lord. But You haven't told me when to expect her. *When* is she coming?"

Soon.

"How will I recognize her? How will I know she's the *one?*"

I'll make it clear. You'll have no doubt.

"I'm looking forward to meeting her."

She's a feisty one. And so lost.

"Then I'll tell her about You."

I'm counting on it, Mary Jo.

Eden Lambert needed a sign. After two full days on the road, she was heartily sick and tired of driving, but she'd committed to press on until she found the exact right place to stop. She'd pulled off the freeway a couple of times over the last forty-eight hours when the name of a town or a glimpse of an area intrigued her, only to reenter the highway minutes later when a pass through the town didn't resonate with her.

She didn't know what she was looking for. But she was confident she'd know it when she saw it.

Honestly, wherever it was, she hoped she'd find it soon. Driving since six this morning with only a couple of potty stops and a quick lunch to break up the monotony, she was hungry and tired and didn't know how much more her backside could take.

A glance in the rearview mirror confirmed Jake had finally fallen asleep in his car seat. He looked like an angel, his lashes fanned out over round pink cheeks and his hair a halo of golden curls. Bless his heart. He'd been such a trooper through all of this, never once complaining. He simply trusted her to care for him.

Love swelled within her. She loved her son with every ounce of her being, and she wouldn't fail him. For his sake she would keep going. No matter how long it took, she'd find a good place for them to settle and start their new lives.

A sign up ahead indicated they were coming to a town. If it looked okay, she'd find a quiet spot to pull over and grab a quick nap while Jake slept.

Some thirty feet from the sign, the words came into focus: *Welcome to Village Green, The Place Where You Belong.* Her breath caught. She blinked to be sure she read it right. Could it be?

She eased off the highway at the flashing yellow light and proceeded slowly down Main Street. A smile stretched across her face. Village Green resembled a tarnished Mayberry from the old black-and-white reruns—a magical place where time moved slowly and relationships mattered.

The two-story, red-brick buildings lining the street looked a bit tired, and many of the stores sat empty and boarded up. But some optimistic soul had set out huge planters at regular intervals along the sidewalk and heaped them with cheerful pink and purple flowers, as though they were acknowledging they'd been through some tough times but looked for better days ahead.

The parallel to her own life was unmistakable.

On the shop side of the street, pretty benches invited passersby to slow down and relax. Across from them was a two-block-long park ringed with a sturdy iron fence and planted with huge beds of colorful flowers and towering trees. Wouldn't Jake love running through the thick grass?

Eden felt a stirring of hope. Maybe this *was* the place where they belonged.

While she drove, she kept an eye out for a place to stop. The on-street parking in front of the shops wouldn't do. Too visible. A woman and child sleeping in the car in plain sight would attract unwanted attention.

She took a right on the first road just past the park into a deeply shaded residential area. Huge old homes lined the narrow street. The second house on the left caught her attention. Set up on a rise, the majestic two-story seemed to beckon her. She followed it with her eyes as far as she could crane her neck, then made a U-turn at the intersection and came back to park in front of it.

A shaft of sunlight speared through the leafy canopy to illuminate the house like a spotlight. Golden rays glinted off the paned window in the door, sparkling like jewels.

Eden rubbed her eyes. Blinking into the bright light exacerbated the gritty feeling of her heavy lids. Maybe they'd just rest here a minute. She lowered the windows a couple of inches for ventilation before shutting down the engine, checked Jake one more time, leaned back against the headrest, and closed her eyes.

An annoying staccato repeated at the edge of her consciousness. *Tap tap tap.* There it was again. Eden reluctantly forced her eyes open to find a twinkling-eyed old woman standing on the passenger side of the car and peering in the window.

"Oh!" Eden sat up with a guilty start. A peek at the dashboard clock said she'd been sleeping for almost half an hour. She glanced back at Jake. He was wide awake and grinning through the window at the smiling woman.

Eden turned the ignition key and lowered the window a bit more before leaning toward the woman and pitching her voice so she could be heard through the opening. "I'm so sorry. Is this your home? I must have fallen asleep for a moment. I'm truly sorry to have bothered you. We'll go." She reached for the gear shifter on the console.

The woman waved her hands and shook her head vigorously. "No, no, please don't leave. You're not bothering me. I've been waiting for you."

Eden blinked. Huh? She must have misheard her. "I'm really embarrassed. I pulled up to admire your home and must have dozed off. Your house is amazing."

"Thank you." The woman looked over her shoulder at the house, and back at Eden. "If you have a minute, why don't you two come in? I'd be happy to give you a tour."

"Oh, no," Eden said. "I wouldn't want to impose."

The woman dismissed her suggestion with a flick of her hand. "It's not an imposition. The house is part of the annual tour of homes. I bring people through all the time."

They had those tours back in Tallahassee too. People bought tickets to tromp through rich people's houses. Eden had thought it would be cool to do someday. Still . . . she frowned. A product of the stranger-danger generation, she'd been raised to keep her distance from people she didn't know.

"I understand if you don't want to come in since you don't know me . . ." The light in her bright blue eyes seemed to dim as her voice trailed off.

Eden was wary but not heartless. The woman was clearly lonely. And honestly, she couldn't be less threatening. She was short and comfortably rounded, and with her tastefully tinted blonde bob and expensive-looking dress, she was the picture of grandmotherly elegance. Like an upscale Aunt Bee.

Besides, this was a once-in-a-lifetime chance to see inside such an incredible home without buying a ticket.

She met Jake's eyes in the rearview mirror. "We'd love a tour, wouldn't we?"

He bobbed his head. "Wuv. Wuv."

She unbuckled her seat belt, picked up her handbag, and climbed out of the car. After indulging in a quick stretch to work out the all-day-in-the-car kinks, she rounded the bumper to introduce herself to the older woman.

She extended her hand. "I'm Eden Lambert."

"I'm so glad to meet you. I'm Mary Jo Piermont." She held Eden's hand an extra moment while she studied her face with a friendly but penetrating gaze. At last she gave Eden's hand a squeeze and released it. "My goodness, what a lovely young lady you are."

"Thank you." Eden stepped across the curb and opened the back door of the sedan. She leaned in to undo the buckles and straps securing her son and lifted him into her arms.

"Jake, this nice lady is Mrs. Piermont."

"Way-dee. Way-dee."

Mrs. Piermont clasped her hands over her heart. "I wasn't expecting a baby. What a surprise."

"You're telling me. We're talking total surprise." Eden nodded. "My boyfriend and I weren't together anymore when I found out I was pregnant."

"Oh." Mrs. Piermont's forehead wrinkled, and her mouth turned down. "I'm so sorry."

Stiffening, Eden lifted her chin. "I'm not."

"Forgive me, dear. I wasn't saying I'm sorry you have a child." Mary Jo smiled. "I'm only sorry because it must be very difficult to raise one alone."

Down girl. The ever-ready fight drained from Eden's body as quickly as it appeared. The woman wasn't judging her. Just empathizing.

Eden exhaled. "Yeah, it's been rough. But totally worth it." She squeezed her son. "Jake and I are a family."

Jake grunted and struggled to be released. Eden lowered him to his feet and took his hand so he wouldn't run into the street.

"You are a precious little family." Mrs. Piermont beamed at both of them. "I'm just so glad you're here. Let's go inside, shall we?" She turned and started up the brick walkway toward the house. "We can have something cool to drink before we begin the tour."

Eden picked up her son and followed her hostess, promising herself they wouldn't drink anything. She may be willing to enter the house of a stranger, but she drew the line at accepting a beverage.

The red brick walkway bisected a perfectly manicured lawn and ended in a wide staircase of the same aged brick. They climbed the stairs to a deep wraparound porch furnished with white rocking chairs and lush potted ferns.

She paused on the top step to take it all in. "It's like something in a magazine."

"That's so sweet of you to say." Mrs. Piermont opened the door and stepped aside for them to enter.

"There's a powder room here to the left." She pointed in that direction. "I'll fix us a glass of tea while you two freshen up, and you can meet me in the kitchen." She gestured toward the back of the house. "What does young Master Jake drink?"

Eden ruffled his curls. "He's an apple juice man. I have his sippy cup here in my purse. It's still half full from lunch. He can drink that."

The interior of the old house surprised Eden. Because of its age, she'd expected it to look stuffy and smell stale. Instead, tall windows framed by flowing drapes filled it with sunlight, and overhead fans whirled lazily to stir the fresh air.

After they made use of the pretty little bathroom, she carried Jake over gleaming hardwood floors, through an elegant living area decorated in the softest shades of blue and green, toward the back of the house.

Eden paused just inside the kitchen. The room was huge, easily half as big as her entire apartment had been, and sunny and bright with gleaming white cabinets and black granite countertops.

"There you are." Mrs. Piermont carried two tall beverages over to the round glass table situated in front of a bay window overlooking the backyard. "Come sit down. I made peach tea today. Do you use any sweetener?"

"No, thank you." Eden sat and settled Jake in her lap before accepting the glass and placing it in front of her. She pulled his cup from her bag and handed it to him. "Your house is amazing."

The older woman took the seat across from her and smiled. "Thank you. I love decorating. I just recently redid the living room. And before that, the kitchen." She leaned forward to confide. "When my husband was alive, he used to say he was afraid to leave for work in the morning for fear he wouldn't recognize the place when he got home that night."

Eden nodded. The dead husband sounded like the kind of man her mother brought home. Well, except for the part about him leaving for work. "Men don't appreciate women."

Mrs. Piermont chuckled at her tone. "Some don't, I'm sure. But the right men do. My Matthew cherished me until the day he died."

"You were one of the lucky ones then."

"I've been blessed, that's for sure."

Eden watched Mrs. Piermont taste her tea. It looked so good, and she was suddenly thirsty. Surely Aunt Bee wouldn't poison a guest. She took a deep breath, lifted her glass, and took a tentative sip. The tea tasted fine, cold and refreshing. She drank again, deeply this time, ashamed of herself for having been suspicious of the hospitality of a sweet, lonely old lady.

"Have you lived here long?"

"Going on sixty years." Mrs. Piermont wagged her head. "Mercy, how time flies. Seems like only yesterday Matthew and I moved in as newlyweds."

Eden let her gaze sweep the oversized kitchen. "This must have been a lot of house for a young couple."

"It was. We inherited it from Matthew's aunt. I had hoped to fill it with children, but it seemed the Lord had other plans." She turned a doting smile on Jake. "Your son is just delightful. I wonder, is there anything dearer than a toddler's chubby hands?"

"They are pretty sweet," Eden said, gathering his fingers in hers. "Except right after he's eaten. He hasn't mastered the whole spoon and fork thing yet, and mealtime gets a bit messy."

Mrs. Piermont's bright blue eyes widened. "Goodness, it's almost dinnertime, isn't it? Since you're here, I hope you'll join me."

Eden shook her head. "That's nice of you to invite us, but after the tour, we need to get back on the road."

"You have to eat," she reasoned. "And since it's Sunday night, everything in Village Green will be closed up tight."

"Oh." Eden frowned. Major downside to Mayberry living. "Well, we'll find something. We wouldn't want to inconvenience you."

"It wouldn't be any trouble. It's such a treat to have company at dinner." She gave Eden a gentle smile. "I won't press you for an answer now. Give it some thought. And if you decide you want to stay, please know you are very welcome here."

You are very welcome here. Were there any sweeter words in the English language? "Thank you."

"Can I get you a refill on your tea?"

Eden shook her head. "No, thanks. I'm good."

"Then let's begin our tour. Since you've seen most of the first floor, we can start upstairs."

Mrs. Piermont led the way out of the kitchen and up a flight of stairs to the second story. She stopped at the room at the far end of the hall and motioned for Eden to enter ahead of her. "This suite is my favorite. The bedroom has the best view of the garden and is connected to a smaller bedroom through the bath."

Eden picked up Jake and stepped inside. The tall ceilings and an entire wall of windows filled the large room with light. "It's beautiful."

"Thank you. Most of the furnishings are antiques. The canopy bed and chest of drawers are mahogany and belonged to Matthew's aunt." Mary Jo pointed while she spoke. "The desk and chair in the corner, also mahogany, were my grandmother's."

Eden carried Jake farther into the room to get a better look. The delicately carved four-poster bed was positioned against the wall facing the windows so the occupant could enjoy the view. A mound of plump pillows and a thick comforter in purest white lay beneath a gauzy canopy of white lace. A pale pink throw folded at the foot of the bed, the rug, and two slipper chairs upholstered in the same rosy shade provided the only hint of color in the room.

She sighed. "I can see why it's your favorite. It looks like a room for a princess."

Her hostess smiled.

After Eden had looked her fill, they stepped back into the hall and walked to the next door. Mrs. Piermont pointed inside. "This is the smallest bedroom. Because of its location, it doesn't get a lot of natural light. When my nephew visits, I like to put him in here." Her hostess giggled with her guilty admission.

"I'm guessing from your expression that he's not a favorite." Eden peeked inside. The room was decorated in comfortable blues and had a more masculine feel, definitely not as large or as lavish as the one they'd just seen. Of course, both rooms were beyond anything she'd ever lived in.

"No, he's not. He lives far enough away that he doesn't come very often, but when he does, I'm careful not to make him too comfortable." Mrs. Piermont chuckled. "He might not want to leave."

This nephew guy was *definitely* like her mother's men. "Freeloader, huh?"

Her hostess cocked her head and pursed her lips. "Part freeloader, part vulture. Todd is my only living relative, my husband's sister's son, and he's counting the days until I die and he can get his hands on this." She lifted her palms to indicate the house.

Eden grimaced. "What a creep. I can see why he's not a favorite. I don't even know him, and I don't like him."

Mrs. Piermont chuckled, eyes twinkling. "I like your plain speaking. I can tell you and I will be good friends."

Two more bedrooms, each with their own bath, completed the tour of the upper story. Jake had taken the first part of the tour with calm acceptance, but by the time they'd seen the primary suite, he'd had enough.

Mrs. Piermont noticed him squirming in his mother's arms. "I don't think Jake is much interested in old houses. Why don't we take him outside where he can run?"

They retraced their steps down the stairs to the back of the house.

Eden knew from looking out the windows that the backyard was planted in formal beds of multicolored flowers. Even so, she wasn't prepared for the breathtaking view when she stepped out through the French doors onto the sprawling flagstone terrace.

Blooms of every color circled the patio area. Beyond the terrace, the gently sloped yard of perfectly trimmed grass featured several smaller beds of flowers and shrubs artfully punctuated with a statue, bird bath, or bench.

Her jaw dropped. "Did you do all of this?"

The older woman nodded. "Matthew and I laid out the beds and did the original plantings. These days I putter around out here, but I have a service to maintain it."

"It's incredible. I've never seen anything like it." Eden's gaze swept the lush property. "It's like Disney World without the crowds."

Mrs. Piermont beamed. "Thank you." She walked to the filigreed iron table and chairs. "We can sit here and let Jake run."

"I think I better stay with him." Eden placed him on the ground and seconds later sprinted to his side and grabbed his hand before he could behead a fistful of red blooms.

"Don't worry," Mrs. Piedmont called. "He can't hurt anything."

Says the woman who's never had children.

Eden and Jake wandered the yard, investigating each of the smaller beds. They tried out benches, sniffed blooms, and admired butterflies. Though the late afternoon had grown warm, the trees edging the property provided comfortable shade.

After a half hour or so, Eden scooped him up and carried him back to the terrace. "I think my friend here needs a diaper change, so this is probably a good time to end our tour. Your home and yard are wonderful. Thank you so much for sharing them with us."

Mrs. Piermont stood. "You are very welcome. But do you really have to leave so soon? We'll have dinner in an hour or so, and I'd love for you to stay. It won't be fancy, but it'll be better than anything you can find on the road. Plus, you won't have to put Jake back into his car seat for a while longer." She smiled at him. "I can tell he's enjoying his freedom."

Eden looked at her son, his face pink from his romp in the grass, his curls damp with perspiration. He'd been cooped up in the car for hours already, and who knew how long it would be before they found a decent place to eat or spend the night? The invitation was tempting.

"Are you sure we won't be in the way?"

Mrs. Piermont nodded. "Absolutely."

Eden smiled. "Then we'd be happy to stay for dinner. If it's okay with you, I'll just run out to the car and get his diaper bag."

"Perfect. While you're outside, I'll head upstairs and spread a towel on the smaller bed in the back suite. You can use that as his changing table."

Jake on her hip, Eden collected the bag from the back seat and reentered the house.

Her hostess met her at the foot of the stairs. "Do you have everything you need?"

"We're good, thanks. We'll be down in a minute."

Joe shifted the grocery bags to one hand so he could let himself into the house. Mary Jo met him at the door, and he bent to kiss her cheek. "Hey, did you know there's a strange car with Florida tags parked in front of your house? I don't know how long it's been there, but I called Sam and asked him to run the plates." He pushed the front door closed behind him.

"Oh, dear." Mary Jo wrung her hands. "Call him back, Joe, and tell him not to bother. The car belongs to my, uh, friend."

He skewered her with a look. "I didn't know you had friends in Florida."

"Oh, sure." Her all-too-angelic expression and the fact she wouldn't meet his eyes said she was 100 percent guilty of something.

What is she up to now?

He looked past her to see a long-legged beauty with a child on her hip appear at the top of the stairs.

"Here they are now." Mary Jo shot him a pleading look before scurrying over to wait for them. "Joe, dear, I want you to meet my friends, Eden and Jake."

He watched with a mixture of appreciation and suspicion as the visitors descended. Appreciation because, as an acknowledged connoisseur of women, he could not deny the fact the tall, golden-tanned blonde was breathtaking. Literally. He felt like he'd been punched in the gut and couldn't fill his lungs.

Suspicion because, as Mary Jo's self-proclaimed protector, he knew without a doubt the stranger was one of Mary Jo's strays.

"Eden, this *gentleman* is Joe Wolfe." Mary Jo placed extra emphasis on the word, probably to recall him to his manners. "Though I don't have any children of my own, Joe is the son of my heart."

The beauty, in worn blue jeans and a gray Florida State T-shirt, stopped at the foot of the stairs and offered him a faint smile and cool nod. "Hello."

He returned the nod, crossed his arms over his chest, and waited.

Clearly uncomfortable, Mary Jo's hands fluttered while she searched for something to say to break the awkward silence he'd initiated. "Aren't they wonderful?"

He ignored the question, giving the twosome a quick, intentionally insulting once-over. "What are they doing here?"

"They're visiting me, of course," Mary Jo said brightly.

He gave them another dismissive glance. "I can see that." He quirked a brow. "Why?"

"Because I asked them to." Mary Jo frowned. "Really, Joe. It's not like you to be so rude." Her gaze traveled to the bags in his hands. "Is that dinner you're carrying?"

"Yes, ma'am."

"Then why don't you take it into the kitchen and get started." She shooed at him with the backs of her hands, her expression mild, but her tone warning him of a scold ahead.

The visitor didn't look flustered or uncomfortable as he'd intended, just resigned. "Maybe we should go," she suggested with a quiet dignity as she took a step toward the door.

Mary Jo laid a gently restraining hand on her arm. "This is my home, and you and Jake are my honored guests." She cast a now-look-what-you've-done scowl at Joe before turning back to her. "Would you like to wait out on the terrace? I'll help Joe get dinner started, then I'll join you."

As the "friends" headed for the backyard, he hefted the groceries and moved to the kitchen with Mary Jo hot on his heels.

"Oh, Joseph. How could you?"

"Easy." He unloaded the contents of the bags onto the counter. "Somebody needs to look after you. If you won't be responsible for your safety, then I'll have to do it."

"My safety?" She tsked derisively.

He faced her, his expression stern to communicate the gravity of the situation. "Tell me, when exactly did you meet these new *friends*?"

She lowered her eyes and shifted her feet. "It's a relatively new acquaintance."

He focused his truth-ray stare on her and waited. He knew from experience she couldn't hold out long.

She raised her gaze to his and huffed. "Fine. I met them this afternoon."

Great. Much worse than he thought. "You invited complete strangers into your home?" He gripped her shoulders. "Honey, what were you thinking? You know nothing about that woman. Did it ever occur to you she might be dangerous? That she could be a criminal?"

Mary Jo clapped her hands to her face in mock horror. "They're probably part of a vicious gang. I bet that sweet baby is not a child at all, but actually her short, evil accomplice."

"Very funny." He swung back to the counter, scooped up the strawberries and green beans, and carried them to the sink. He turned on the faucet to wash them. "I'm serious, Mary Jo. You are entirely too trusting."

She stood on tippy toes to open the cabinet beside him and took out four plates. The fact she was willing to set the table said Mary Jo knew she was in trouble and was trying to placate him. "Perhaps. But you're not trusting enough. I've always said you were too cynical."

He washed a handful of strawberries and placed them on a paper towel to dry. "If you think you're going to turn this conversation on me, you're wrong."

"I'm sorry, dear." She set the plates on the table. "I just think you're making too much of a simple invitation to dinner."

He shut off the water to give her his full attention. "She was coming downstairs when I arrived. Since when does a dinner guest wander through your house? She was probably casing the place."

Mary Jo paused at the drawer where she kept the napkins, a deep frown on her face. "I probably shouldn't tell you about the tour."

Torn between the desire to laugh or scream, he placed his hands on the countertop, rolled his eyes toward the ceiling, and huffed a long-suffering sigh. "Mary Jo."

"You've got to stop watching so much television. It's making you suspicious of everyone."

He faced her. "It's not television. It's reality. Listen to me. You don't know this woman. Even if she didn't have plans to harm you physically, she could be a thief. How would you feel if you came home one day and the place was cleared out?"

She carried the napkins to the table and positioned them just so beside the plates. "A certain sense of relief, I think, as long as she was tidy about it." She turned to look at him. "Think, dear. Even a robbery has a silver lining. There'd be less for Todd to take."

He ground his teeth. He didn't know how they'd gotten so far off course from the original topic. Worse, he didn't know how to communicate to her just how dangerous her actions were. "I need you to hear me. You cannot invite complete strangers into your home. It's not safe."

Her sly smile said she had an ace to play. "What if I told you she's not a complete stranger?"

"I'd say you were trying to pull one over on me." He narrowed his eyes. "And, I might add, not for the first time."

"No, it's true. I didn't tell you before because I know you don't take this sort of thing well, but I knew she was coming."

He quirked a brow and folded his arms across his chest. "Oh yeah? How?"

"God told me."

His heart sank to his toes. He crossed to her, capturing her lined face in his hands and gently turning it up to his. "Please don't say crazy stuff like that. It's just the kind of thing Todd is looking for to have you declared mentally incompetent. If he got wind of this, he'd have you locked up so fast—"

She covered his hands with hers and smiled at him. "Todd can't hurt me. Not when I have you as my champion."

He dropped a quick kiss on her forehead. "Nice try. It's too late to sweet-talk me."

"It's the absolute truth. I'm not worried when I have you to keep me safe."

"I'm glad you have so much faith in me." He returned to the sink and his food prep. "Now see if you can stop making my job so difficult."

She paused in the doorway. "I'll try. In return, will you please be nice to our dinner guests?"

He could probably manage to tolerate them for an hour. "I'll try."

CHAPTER TWO

Mrs. Piermont hurried out onto the terrace to the table where Eden sat with Jake. "I'm so sorry. I don't know what came over Joe." She looked toward the back door and frowned. "He's usually so charming. Maybe he's annoyed with me because I didn't warn him that we had company for dinner. Cooks can be so temperamental."

Eden's brows shot to her hairline. "He's your chef?"

"Not officially, of course." She took the seat next to Eden. "I quit cooking after my husband died. There wasn't any point in preparing a big meal for myself, so I started buying those little frozen dinners. They really aren't too bad. But Joe found out, and the next thing you know he's at my door with a bag full of groceries offering to fix me a meal." She smiled. "Isn't he the sweetest thing?"

There were many words Eden could use to describe Mr. Hospitality, but *sweet* didn't make the list. Luckily, Mrs. Piermont didn't wait for her response.

"Over the years, we've settled into a schedule of sorts. He cooks on Sunday, Tuesday, and Thursday, and I have plenty of leftovers for the rest of the time."

"Why Sunday, Tuesday, and Thursday?"

"That leaves his weekends free. I didn't want to interfere with his social life." She leaned in and whispered with obvious pride, "Joe's very popular with the ladies."

"His type always is."

Mrs. Piermont must have heard the disgust in her voice. "I'm sorry he's given you such a poor impression. He's really very sweet," she said. "And handsome. You probably didn't notice because he was so rude. He'll just have to apologize."

She *had* noticed how handsome he was. She'd have had to be blind to miss it. He was tall and muscularly lean with the perfectly sculpted features and dark, wavy hair of one of those models in the cologne ads. His eyes were dark and heavily lashed, and his white smile, what little she saw of it, was movie star quality. There may have even been a dimple.

The drop-dead looks, the casual arrogance in his stance, even the way he wore his snug, faded jeans and T-shirt proclaimed his bad boy status. Eden had no doubt he was popular with the ladies, which was all the more reason to avoid him.

She might be a poor judge of men, but even she knew a bad boy was bad news.

Eden smiled at her hostess. "He doesn't need to apologize." In fact, he didn't need to speak to her. Ever.

Though she'd taken him and his cockiness into instant dislike, he did appear to have one redeeming quality. His earlier impersonation of a bristling Doberman was obviously his way of looking out for the woman who thought of him as a son. "He thinks he's protecting you."

Mrs. Piermont propped her elbows on the table, sunk her chin in her hands, and sighed. "I don't understand why he thinks I need protecting."

Oh boy. Where to start? She was old. She lived alone. Wealthy and generous and trusting enough to let complete strangers roam her home, sweet Mrs. Piermont was a crime waiting to happen.

"You are a kind and generous person, Mrs. Piermont," Eden said, feeling very much like the worldly-wise parent trying to coach her naïve child.

"What a lovely thing to say. But I wish you would call me Mary Jo."

"Sure. Thank you." She paused, searching for the right way to alert Mary Jo to potential threats without frightening her. The point was to make her aware, not fearful. She looked down at her hands while she carefully chose each word. "There are bad people out there who prey on the unsuspecting. You need to be cautious."

Eden glanced up to see how her warning was received. It wasn't. Rather than listening to her advice, her hostess's attention was fully focused on Jake who sat at their feet, playing with her car keys. Clearly, Mary Jo hadn't heard a word Eden said.

She had a moment's sympathy for Joe. Keeping this woman out of trouble would be a full-time job.

Mary Jo looked over at Eden and patted her hand. "I think we've talked enough about me. While we're waiting for dinner, I want to hear all about you and your dear little man."

Subject closed.

Eden vowed to bring it up again before she left. She didn't know why, but in the short time they'd been together, Mary Jo had become important to her. She wanted to know Mary Jo was safe.

She shrugged. "There's not much to tell. I'm twenty-four years old. Jake is eighteen months. We lived in Florida, in Tallahassee, with my mom until . . ." She paused. She didn't want to withhold the truth from her hostess, but she didn't want to paint her mother in a bad light either. "Things got crowded, so Jake and I decided it was time to find our own place and make a fresh start."

Something about the sympathetic look in Mary Jo's eyes said she understood how wrenching the decision had been. "Texas is a long way from Tallahassee."

"Yeah. I didn't plan to come so far, but once I got behind the wheel, I just didn't see a good place to stop." She thought about the self-doubts she'd battled with every mile, the ever-present temptation to turn back, and the knowledge there was nowhere to go back to. "Before I knew it, the miles had racked up, and we'd made it to Texas."

Mary Jo nodded and leaned in. "Tell me what brought you to Village Green? We're quite a bit off the beaten path."

She folded her hands on the table and sighed. "This is going to sound silly." She looked down and then at Mary Jo. "To begin with, I want you to know I'm not usually the superstitious type. I'm all about common sense. But as I was driving along, I was waiting for a sign, you know, some indication that we'd arrived where we were supposed to go."

Mary Jo's gently affirming smile and nod said she didn't see anything weird about her plan. In fact, the look she gave Eden said it all made perfect sense. *Really, the woman is so nonjudgmental and easy to talk to.*

"There's this road sign on the highway just outside of town that says, *Welcome to Village Green, The Place Where You Belong.* Something about it felt right, so I pulled off to take a closer look. Jake was napping, and I was suddenly so sleepy . . ." Eden laughed. "Well, you know the rest since you found us dozing in your front yard."

"What an adventure." Mary Jo placed her hands over her heart and sighed. "I'm so glad God brought you to me." She glanced from

Jake to Eden. "You know, I think Village Green would be a wonderful place for you and Jake to live."

Eden returned her smile. "I like what I've seen so far."

She and Mary Jo fell into easy conversation, like a couple of old friends, while Jake entertained himself at their feet. It seemed like no time before Joe appeared at the door and waved them back to the house.

Her hostess waved in response. "Oh good, dinner must be ready. Joe made us his chicken Marsala tonight. I know it will be delicious. I hope you're hungry."

"Starved." Good thing too. Because nothing short of starvation would induce her to share a meal with *him*, no matter how much her hostess loved the man. Was it too much to hope he prepared the meal and wouldn't stay to eat?

Mary Jo glanced down at Jake. "What are we going to do with this little one? I'd hate for you to have to hold him on your lap during dinner. Do you think he would sit on a chair to eat?"

"I have a portable high chair for him in the car." Eden scooped him up and extracted her now-spitty keys from his fist. "I'll run and get it."

"We could send Joe."

"Not a chance." Eden shot a look in his direction and shook her head.

Her hostess threw back her head and laughed. "It's going to take a really good apology for him to get into your good graces. Why don't you at least leave Jake with me, so you don't have to carry him *and* the chair up the stairs." She pressed her lips together while she studied him. "Do you think he'll let me hold him?"

Eden glanced at her son, trying to gauge his receptiveness. "I'm not sure. Sometimes he's a little shy."

Mary Jo tentatively reached out her arms, and Jake practically leapt from his mother to her.

Eden laughed. "So much for shyness."

Mary Jo beamed. "Maybe he likes me."

Her wistful tone melted Eden's heart. She smiled. "I think so. You've obviously got the touch."

"He's the sweetest thing." She hugged him to her chest. "An absolute angel."

"And heavy." He could easily topple the older woman. "Can you carry him all the way to the house or would you rather I did?"

Mary Jo tightened her grip on him and shook her head. It was clear she had no intention of releasing her prize. "I've got him. You run and get the high chair."

Joe stood in the doorway, arms folded across his chest, waiting.

"You can go around the side of the house if you want to," Mary Jo whispered.

Eden nodded. "Good plan. See you two inside."

Mary Jo still held Jake when Eden reentered the house several minutes later and was engaged in a whispered conversation with Joe. Probably trying to get him to back off, at least for dinner.

Good luck with that.

"Where do you want me to put the chair?" she called, giving them a heads-up to her presence.

"Here you are." Mary Jo stepped away from Joe and moved toward the table where they'd had tea earlier. "Let's put it here, between you and me."

Eden unfolded the high chair and positioned it between the two chairs. She took her son from Mary Jo, placed him in the seat, and clicked the plastic tray in place.

He pounded the tray with delight. "More. More."

Eden and Mary Jo laughed.

Joe carried the food over from the stove and placed it in the center of the table. Eden took the seat across from Mary Jo, with Joe to her left.

"Let me ask for the Lord's blessing," Mary Jo said, "then we can eat." Unfamiliar with the practice, Eden was horrified to discover a blessing required they all hold hands. Mary Jo extended hers, one to Joe and one to Jake.

Jake laughed as though it was a wonderful game. "Hand. Hand." Taking Jake's hand was fine, but . . .

Joe must have noticed her hesitation. "Don't worry. I don't bite." His hand rested on the table, palm up, waiting to take hers.

"Couldn't prove it by me." She looked at him, waiting a beat before reluctantly placing her hand in his. His long, cool fingers closed lightly over hers.

Mary Jo bowed her head and closed her eyes. Joe bowed his head. Eden didn't bother to check whether he closed his eyes or not. She lowered her head a fraction, out of respect, but she kept her eyes open so she'd know what to do next.

Mary Jo prayed, "Heavenly Father, thank You for bringing us together this evening. I thank You especially for Eden and Jake. What a treat it is for us all to be together. Would You bless this food and our fellowship? In Jesus's precious name. Amen."

"Amen." Joe dropped her hand with enough haste to communicate his disgust.

Two could play at that game. She shot him a tight smile, then picked up her napkin and made an obvious show of wiping her left hand.

"More. More." Jake banged his tray, reminding her that he hadn't eaten.

Dinner smelled amazing and looked like a feast. There were mashed potatoes, green beans, a platter of chicken breasts smothered in mushrooms and some delicious-smelling sauce, and a heaping bowl of fresh strawberries. Eden hoped no one heard her stomach growl.

Unsure how to proceed, she waited until Mary Jo picked up the bowl of potatoes, placed a serving on her plate, and passed the bowl to Eden.

Eden placed a good-sized helping of everything on her plate, passed the bowls to Joe without meeting his eyes, then transferred a portion of her food to her son's tray. She cut his strawberries into smaller pieces while Jake picked up potatoes with his fingers and pushed them into his mouth with a happy hum. A fistful of strawberries followed.

Mary Jo's face lit with delight. "He's such a good eater. Look at him gobble up those strawberries. Let me help you cut some up for him so you'll have a chance to eat your dinner."

"Thank you." Eden reached over to drop a few more green beans on his tray. "Keeping him fed is a full-time job."

"Where's his father?" Joe asked.

Mary Jo sent him a fierce scowl. "Mercy, Joe. I thought we agreed you would be pleasant during dinner. I think we need to work on your manners."

Jake looked up from his tray and smiled through a mask of mashed potatoes. "Mercy, Joe."

Joe lifted his palms and shrugged. "It's a fair question. How do we know she hasn't snatched the kid? She could be a fugitive with an angry parent or husband in hot pursuit."

Face burning, Eden turned to him. In deference to her hostess, she kept her voice calm and pleasant. "For that matter, I could be from outer space. I might be the first scout of an alien army coming to colonize the earth."

Mary Jo got into the spirit of things. "Or maybe you're a beautiful princess with amnesia."

"Ha ha. You two are a riot." He leveled a stare at Eden. "How about the truth? If you can manage it."

She ignored him, delivering her remarks to Mary Jo instead. "His father and I split shortly after I got pregnant. We weren't married, and as far as I know, he is unaware of Jake. I certainly never told him." She finished by glaring at Joe. "Put your suspicious little mind at ease. We are not running, and there is no one in pursuit."

He returned his attention to his plate. "I guess we can thank heaven for small mercies."

"I thank heaven they've come." Mary Jo turned to Eden. "It's getting late, and you must be tired. Why don't you spend the night here? That way you can get a good look at the town in the daylight to see if it's the right place for you and Jake to settle."

The offer was tempting. She and Jake were both weary, and they'd be safer here than in some sketchy motel. Still. Eden put down her fork and shook her head. "Oh, no, that's very nice, but we won't be staying."

Mary Jo's brows drew together. "Where will you go? Village Green has no hotels."

"There's a motel about fifteen miles south on the highway," Joe said. "I bet they have a room."

Mary Jo shot him a quelling look before turning back to Eden. "There's no reason for you to go to a nasty motel when I have all this room right here. I put fresh sheets on the bed in the back suite just this morning."

"You've already been so kind. I don't want to inconvenience you anymore. And as Joe has pointed out," Eden sent him a glare, "as often and rudely as possible, we are strangers."

Her hostess shook her head. "You are neither inconvenient nor strangers. You and Jake are treasures. Two beautiful, special people God has brought to my door. I want you to stay. I can show you around Village Green tomorrow."

Treasures. Eden blinked back a surprise rush of tears. Funny, it wasn't nastiness but kindness that breached her defenses. "Thank you. If you're sure we won't be a burden, we'd be happy to stay."

"Lovely." Joe packed a lot of sarcasm into the word. He looked at Mary Jo. "You've still got two empty bedrooms. I wonder if there's anybody at the bus station you can invite over?"

Mary Jo's eyes sparkled with mischief. "What a good idea. Eden, remind me and we'll take a pass through there tomorrow and see who we can pick up."

Joe cleared the table while Mary Jo took her guests upstairs. He stacked the plates and silverware and carried them to the sink. He rinsed them thoroughly, then arranged them in the dishwasher. He collected the serving bowls on the counter, placing the leftovers in separate plastic containers to store in the refrigerator.

There wasn't a whole lot left. The blonde and her kid put away a lot of food. He didn't know how much the boy actually ingested and how much just stuck to his face. Joe grimaced. If he hadn't already sworn off the idea of a family, one look at Jake with food smeared everywhere would be enough to put him off children forever.

He filled one side of the double sink with soapy water to finish the pans. Miss Florida was tough. He had to give her credit. She didn't look it, with her big blue eyes and delicate features, but beneath that killer bod was a backbone of steel. It would take strength, certainly, to survive alone—just her and the boy. In some small way he admired her—though not enough to want her to stick around.

At least he knew she didn't present a physical threat to Mary Jo. Before they'd sat down to dinner, Sam had texted the information he'd received from running the license plates on her car. The ten-year-old Honda was registered to one Eden Anne Lambert of Tallahassee, Florida. Her insurance was valid and her driver's license current. The twenty-four-year-old had no unpaid fines or outstanding warrants. According to Sam's information, she'd never even had a speeding ticket.

So, she was an upstanding citizen. He took a measure of comfort from that. At least she wasn't likely to carve up Mary Jo with a butcher knife or rob her while she slept.

His queries over dinner answered his other big questions. He'd needed to know if she was on the run and whether they could expect somebody showing up on their doorstep looking for her. Neither Mary Jo nor he needed that kind of drama in their lives. If his method of collecting information seemed unnecessarily harsh, he wasn't sorry.

He grinned. She'd been blazing mad, her eyes shooting icy blue daggers at him across the dinner table, and holding back from telling him off.

He didn't care what she thought. As long as she knew he was watching her, and Mary Jo wasn't some unprotected old lady, he'd done his job.

His hostess trundled into the room. "Well, Joseph, I hope you're proud of yourself."

He was always Joseph, not Joe, when he was in trouble. He swung around to face her, choosing to deliberately misunderstand. "I am. I thought dinner turned out really well. Of course, had I known we had company, I'd have brought more."

She narrowed her eyes. "Now who's trying to pull one over on whom? You know perfectly well I am referring to your inexcusable treatment of Eden. What on earth would possess you to be so unkind? I swear, I'm positively ashamed of you."

That hurt. Mary Jo was the closest thing he'd had to a mother, and her opinion mattered more to him than anything.

He stiffened. "I'm sorry if you don't approve of my methods—"

"*Methods?*" She slapped her hands on her hips. "Was it your *method* to shame and humiliate a brave young woman doing the best she can for herself and her son?"

He shrugged. "She's no Twinkie. It would take more than a round of hardball to shame and humiliate her."

"She *is* strong, isn't she?" Never one to stay mad, Mary Jo was back to all smiles. "The Lord warned me she'd be feisty."

He lifted his palms to stop her. "Whoa. Nope. Let's don't go there. You know I don't want to hear the woo-woo talk."

"Fine. But I like her." She grinned. "And I believe you'll come to like her too."

He turned back to the pans waiting in the sink. He picked up the pot he'd used to boil the potatoes and scrubbed it with a sponge. "Don't hold your breath. First of all, she won't be here long enough for me to grow to like her. Secondly, she's the very thing I've sworn to avoid."

"I've never known you to avoid an attractive woman before."

He rinsed the pot and set it on the dish towel he'd spread on the counter. "It's not the looks I'm opposed to. It's the kid. You know I'm not a family man, and she comes with one ready-made. The fact she's beautiful means nothing to me."

Mary Jo smiled and nodded. "She's lovely, isn't she? When she climbed out of the car, she positively stole my breath. And that figure. I'm sure I've never seen a better one." Her voice turned sly. "I wondered what you'd think of her."

"Wonder no more because I'm not going to think of her." He plunked another clean pan on the towel. "Ever."

She gave a knowing chuckle. "Famous last words."

He glanced at her over his shoulder. "I'm serious. You do what you feel you need to do for her—like you were waiting for my permission—then send her on her way. The sooner, the better." He finished washing the last pot and laid it beside the others. "Since I'm reasonably sure she doesn't pose a threat to you, I'll make myself scarce."

Mary Jo moved to his side. "Not *too* scarce, I hope. You'll come by for dinner on Tuesday and Thursday, won't you?"

"Should I be afraid you're only keeping me around for my cooking?" He pulled a second dish towel out of the drawer, dried the pans, and put them away in the cupboard. He turned to her with a smile. "Don't worry, I won't abandon you entirely, or you'll be feeding your feisty friend and the kid frozen dinners."

"They're really not too bad. Especially the lasagna."

"I'll have to take your word for it." After hanging the damp towels on the handle of the oven door to dry, he wrapped his arm around her shoulders and started toward the front door.

She frowned. "Are you leaving so soon?"

"Yeah, I've got stuff to do at my place, and you've got company upstairs to see to."

She sighed. "It's nice to have people in the house."

Her words broke his heart. She and Matthew had been so close that Mary Jo missed her late husband every single day. He gave her arm a light squeeze. "Funny, you never say that when Todd's here."

She snorted. "Todd is a toad."

They both laughed.

Joe slowed to a stop in the entry hall. He placed both hands on her shoulders and looked down into her eyes. "Don't come outside. Just wave to me from the door. And I want you to close it and lock it before I drive away."

"Yes, mother."

He wagged his head. "I don't know who is feistier, the blonde or you."

She grinned. "Thank you for dinner. It was delicious."

He bent to kiss her cheek. "You're welcome. Call me if you need anything. Otherwise, I plan to be here Tuesday."

"Good night." She waited until he'd taken a few steps out onto the porch. "And I don't just keep you around for your cooking."

He stopped at the top of the stairs and turned. "Oh, yeah?"

She nodded. "I keep you around because you are the light of my life. And even when you have the manners of a warthog, I am still so very proud of you."

He'd never be too old to hear those words. "Buttering me up again?"

"Absolutely. I love you, Joe."

"I love you, too, Mary Jo. Good night."

Eden heard a light tap on the bedroom door. "Yes?"

"It's me, Mary Jo."

"Come in."

The older woman stopped just inside the darkened room. She pitched her voice a notch above a whisper. "I didn't want to disturb you, but I wanted to be sure you had everything you need."

"Oh, my goodness, yes." Eden sat up in the four-poster bed. "I feel like royalty." She ran a hand over the mattress. "What did you do to these sheets to make them feel so soft and silky?"

Mary Jo grinned. "Aren't they just decadent? It's the thread count. I don't remember the exact number, but it was something off the charts."

"They're amazing." Eden sighed. "I may never get out of bed."

Mary Jo chuckled. "I hope you'll sleep in as long as you like."

Another deep sigh. "If only I could get Jake to agree with you."

"I guess babies are early risers." Her hostess glanced in the direction of his room. "Is he asleep already? I'm sorry I missed saying good night."

Eden nodded. "His head touched the crib, and he was out." She pushed back the covers and climbed out of bed. "There's nothing sweeter than a sleeping baby. Come on, let's peek at him."

They crossed the shadowed room into the bathroom. Eden switched off the overhead light and gently eased open the door into the adjoining bedroom.

A night-light cast enough glow to outline Jake's small jammie-clad body sprawled in the bottom of the Pack 'n Play. He was still, the gentle cadence of his breathing and the whirr of the ceiling fan the only sounds in the room.

Eden stood at Mary Jo's side in the bathroom doorway while they enjoyed the peaceful moment. Finally, she eased the door closed and led them back into her room.

Mary Jo placed a hand over her heart and tears sparkled in her eyes. "He is the dearest thing I've ever seen."

Eden nodded. "If we've had a particularly tough day, I'll go into his room after he's asleep just to watch him. It helps to remind me it's all worth it."

Her hostess laid a gentle hand on her shoulder and looked up into her eyes. "You're doing a great job with him. He's very blessed to have such a devoted mother."

Eden's face warmed with pleasure. She'd received more affirmation in the few hours since she'd met this woman than she'd had in her entire life. "Thank you. And thank you, too, for taking up for me at dinner. It's not that I couldn't handle Joe, but it was nice to have someone in my corner."

"I know exactly what you mean." Mary Jo walked toward the door. She stopped and turned to Eden. "May I ask you a question?"

Eden braced herself. They'd talked briefly about Jake's father earlier, but she'd been deliberately vague about the details. Mary Jo had opened her home to them. She was entitled to some answers about the kind of people she had under her roof.

"Sure."

"Do you know Jesus?"

Huh? She'd been so focused on her story, the explanation she would give for her past decisions, she almost missed the out-of-left-field question. She blinked. "Excuse me?"

Mary Jo smiled and repeated. "Do you know Jesus?"

"The religious guy?" Eden shook her head. "No, not really. I mean, I've heard of Him, of course. A neighbor took me to Sunday school a couple of times when I was a kid, and they talked about Him there." Since she could tell it meant a lot to Mary Jo, she added, "He sounded nice."

Her hostess nodded. "He *is* nice. The reason I mention Him is that as a follower of His, I have His promise He will never leave me or forsake me. He's always in my corner."

"That's pretty cool."

"I'd love to talk with you about what it means to be a Jesus follower." Mary Jo smiled. "It has made my life so full of joy and meaning. I believe God brought you and Jake here because He wants to do the same thing for you."

Eden thought about her life. Honestly, at its core, it was nothing more than a struggle for survival. "I could definitely use some joy and meaning."

"We all could. It's late, and I can see you're exhausted. We'll talk about Jesus later. You get to bed and sleep, and I'll see you in the morning." Mary Jo stepped into the hall. "Sweet dreams, dear one."

"Okay. Thank you for everything. And good night." Eden pushed the door closed and crossed to the bed. She climbed in and pulled the amazing sheets up to her chin. While she stared at the lacy canopy overhead, she replayed the highlights of her extraordinary day. Endless road trip. The feeling she should stop in Village Green. Vivacious Mary Jo and her warm hospitality. Relentless Joe and his insults.

She thought about what Mary Jo had said—that God brought her and Jake here. Was it possible? Would He go to all that trouble for a college dropout and her fatherless baby? She drifted off to sleep with a smile on her lips.

CHAPTER THREE

Joe woke with a smile and a sense of anticipation. Not a woo-woo sense, like that spiritual stuff Mary Jo liked to talk about. He chuckled. He didn't know how one person could inspire such love and frustration at the same time. He loved her with every fiber of his being, but there were times when she made him want to pull his hair out.

She and Matthew had both been into spiritual stuff. They went to church all the time, read their Bibles, and talked Jesus day and night. They were also the two finest people he'd ever known, and he suspected their goodness was a direct by-product of their religion.

The religion thing worked for them. It just wasn't for him.

He took a quick shower and dressed in a T-shirt and his last clean pair of jeans—his version of business casual. Thanks to Matthew's generosity and willingness to teach a lonely kid everything he knew about finances and investing, and what Matthew called Joe's gift for numbers, he didn't have to punch a time clock Monday through Friday. Fact was, he didn't have to work at all. At twenty-nine, he'd amassed an investment portfolio that could see him comfortably through the rest of his life.

Not that he intended to quit working. Matthew had instilled in him the belief that work was a blessing and privilege, and he'd been right. Hard work felt good. Putting himself out there, giving his best, made him feel like he mattered. Beyond the satisfaction of a job well done, it gave him the sense his life counted for something. The nicest thing about his financial situation was the freedom to pick and choose his work. The last month or so, he'd spent his time sprucing up the town. His friend Trey and Trey's fiancée had come up with a plan to revitalize Village Green and attract new people and businesses to the area.

Joe owned a lot of real estate along Main Street and had contributed his might to the project by cleaning up and repainting the storefronts and second-floor apartments. As a bonus, if the plan worked, he'd have tenants for the spaces and rents for his bank account.

He snorted a laugh. The plan *had* worked. Village Green had attracted its first two recruits. The blonde and her baby.

If he believed Mary Jo's theory, God brought them to town. *Yeah, right.* More likely she saw the pretty flowers in the two-ton pots he'd nearly sprung a hernia lifting and decided it was a cute place to spend the day.

Village Green wouldn't hold her. He couldn't honestly say he knew her type, but he figured Florida and the kid would be moving on to a place with more people and opportunities. That's what he would do. He just hoped she'd go without breaking Mary Jo's heart.

He wondered how she was doing this morning. Mary Jo, not the blonde. Maybe he'd take a quick pass by her house to look things over.

He fired up his truck to make the two-block trip to Mary Jo's place. He hadn't intentionally moved so close, but when the big old house went on the market three years ago, he picked up the undervalued property as an investment. Somewhere in the process of updating it, he'd decided not to sell.

A psychiatrist would have a heyday with the irrational choice. He didn't need the space. He didn't enjoy the yardwork, and the behemoth was a money pit. On paper, he couldn't justify keeping it. But he did it anyway.

Maybe because it reminded him of Matthew and Mary Jo's home and subconsciously he was trying to re-create the peaceful, joy-filled environment he'd found there. Possibly, he kept it because the house was the polar opposite of the dilapidated shack he'd known growing up. A shrink would no doubt tell him he used the property to obliterate the painful memories of his childhood.

More likely, he'd bought and kept the old place, one of the largest in Village Green, just to show off. To rub the noses of the many naysayers in his success.

Whatever, the house belonged to him. As a bonus, he liked the accessibility to Mary Jo. After Matthew died, it was up to him to care for her.

He backed down the driveway and out onto the tree-lined street. He rounded the corner to Mary Jo's street, and his heart shot to his throat. A police car sat in front of her house.

His mouth went sawdust dry.

He jammed the gas pedal to the floor and made the short block in seconds. He screeched into the driveway, killed the engine, and flew up the stairs, two at a time.

He burst through the door, his breath coming in short pants. "Hello! Mary Jo?"

"We're in here."

Adrenaline propelled him to the kitchen, his heart hammering as a million horrible scenarios played in his head.

He stopped short, bracing his hands on the doorframe to survey the scene. "What's going on?"

His friend, Sam, looked up from the table where he sat with an apparently hale and hearty Mary Jo. "What's up with you, nervous Nellie? You look like you've seen a ghost."

Joe could barely hear him over the pounding in his chest. "What are you doing here? I saw your car parked outside, and I nearly had a heart attack."

Sam used his coffee cup to gesture around the peaceful, sun-filled room. "What does it look like? I'm making a routine call to check on one of my favorite citizens."

"Did *you* call him?" Joe directed his question to Mary Jo who was bouncing the kid on her lap.

She shook her head. "No, dear. But Sam knows he's always welcome." She reached over and patted the cop's hand. "I miss the days when you boys used to gather around the table and try to eat us out of house and home."

"Mary Jo's friend whipped up a batch of fresh blueberry muffins and was nice enough to invite me to stay." Sam grinned. "We're just waiting until they come out of the oven."

Now that he'd calmed down, he could smell something delicious baking. "Where is Mary Jo's *friend*?"

"She ran upstairs to get some cereal for Jake," Mary Jo said. "She'll be back down in a minute."

Joe took two steps into the kitchen and lowered his voice. "So, Sam, why are you *really* here?"

Sam's grin stretched until it nearly split his face. "Are you kidding? I came to check out your perp. Does the cryptic message 'she looks like trouble' ring a bell? You were so freaked out about Mary Jo's guest, I figured it wouldn't hurt to stop by. You know, be sure everything is on the up-and-up."

Now that his heart rate was normalizing, he felt a little foolish. "I wasn't freaked out."

"If I recall correctly, the phrase 'possible murderer' was bandied about."

A lot foolish. "Well, I—"

Mary Jo nodded. "It's true. Joe was convinced Eden was a gang member or a burglar. He actually accused her to her face of being a kidnapper."

"Nuh-uh, dude, did you really?" Sam's expression was a cross between wonder and horror. "Where's all that legendary charm I'm always hearing about?"

"I was being cautious." He heard the light footfalls and sensed Eden's arrival behind him.

"He was being a horse's patoot," she said.

Jake giggled. "Patoot."

Joe turned slowly toward her and *Bam!* He hadn't imagined her incredible looks or the impact they had on his solar plexus. His gaze drifted downward, and his eyes nearly fell out of his head. What in the world was she wearing? A white tank top and the tiniest shorts he'd ever seen. She'd thrown a men's dress shirt over the ensemble, to act as a robe. In no part of the world would that be considered even remotely modest.

She pushed her long blonde braid over her shoulder. "Are you here to see if I'd looted the place during the night?"

He dragged his eyes back to her face and cleared his throat. Twice. "I'm here because I saw a cop car out front, and I was worried."

"Oh." Her expression softened. "Well, we're fine. Your friend Sam just came by to say hi and welcome us to Texas. Isn't that sweet?" She padded over to the oven on tanned, slender feet, the shirt swishing across the backs of her thighs.

Sam's eyes nearly bugged out of his head when she bent to check the progress of her muffins. "That's Sam all right," Joe said. "Sweet."

Sam nodded, his eyes never wavering from her crouching form. "Sweet."

"If you're free, maybe you can stay and eat with us." Mary Jo pointed to a chair.

"No, he can't stay. He's got work to do." Sam made a shooing motion with his hands. "Run along, Joe."

"Yeah, you know what? I've got a minute or two to spare this morning." Joe pulled out a chair across from Sam and smirked. "I'd love a muffin."

Apparently unaware of the disturbance she and her mile-long legs created, Eden opened the oven door and removed the pan. "We'll let them cool a minute, then we can eat. In the meantime, I'll put Jake in the high chair and get him started on some cereal."

"Let me." Sam lifted the kid from Mary Jo's arms and gently placed him in the seat. "He's really cute."

Joe cocked a brow at his friend's uncharacteristic behavior. "And you *like* babies, do you, Sam?"

"Oh, sure." In response to Joe's stare, Sam shrugged. "Well, I haven't actually been this close to many babies, but Jake here is great."

Eden flashed him a heart-stopping smile when she moved beside him to click the tray in position and scatter Cheerios over it. "Thank you, Sam."

He smiled back, his eyes vaguely unfocused, and his head bobbing mindlessly.

"Breathe, buddy," Joe whispered to his friend. "Breathe."

Her hands now free, Mary Jo stood. "Can I get you a cup of coffee, Joe?"

"No, thanks." He waved her back to her chair. "You stay there. I'll get it." He hopped up from the table, snagged a mug from the cabinet, and filled it from the pot on the coffeemaker. He propped a hip against the counter and took a cautious sip. "Good coffee, Mary Jo."

"Eden made it."

"You've been a busy little bee this morning, haven't you?" Since Eden didn't bother to look at him, she missed the sneer he aimed in her direction.

"Jake and I are early risers." She gently removed the muffins from the pan, placed them on a plate, carried them over to the table, and set them in the center. "I hope you all like them."

The kid's blue eyes rounded when he spied the treats. "More. More." He smacked his tray for emphasis, launching the Cheerios into the air.

Mary Jo laughed. She took a muffin from the plate and peeled back the paper. "I'll cut him a piece of this one, if it's okay with you?"

Eden nodded and took her seat. "Sure. He loves them."

Eden didn't take one. Instead, she sat on the edge of her chair, lips compressed, watching closely as Sam and Mary Jo took their first bites.

Sam closed his eyes and chewed with noisy ecstasy. "Oh man, these are amazing."

Mary Jo nodded. "This has to be the best thing I've ever put in my mouth."

Jake hummed his approval.

Eden relaxed into the chair and took a deep breath.

"I'm so glad," she said. "I've been experimenting with the recipe for a while."

"Your work is done." Sam nodded to her between bites. "They're perfect."

"That's high praise, coming from a man who thinks pastries are one of the essential food groups." Curious, Joe reached across the table and grabbed one. He pulled off the wrapper and took a big bite.

Wow. Amazing. He'd thought the others were flattering her, but they spoke the absolute truth. The warm, fragrant muffin melted in his mouth. He caught himself before he started humming his pleasure like little Jake. He faced her. "They *are* really good."

Amusement danced in eyes the same clear shade of blue as her son's. "Surprised?"

"Impressed." He reached for a second one. "Where'd you learn to bake like this?"

"I worked in a bakery in Tallahassee."

Sam lifted the plate to her. "Eden, you need to try one before they're gone."

She sent him an easy smile. "Thank you."

The muffins were gone in minutes. Joe stopped after two, though he would have cheerfully eaten more. Sam polished off the rest while lingering over his coffee and stealing glances at Eden. Poor guy was clearly smitten.

Joe finished his coffee and stood. "That was excellent. Thank you," he said to the table at large. "I need to get going. Come on, officer, and I'll walk you to your car."

Sam looked away from Eden just long enough to glance up at him and frown. "You go ahead. I was thinking about one more cup of coffee before I head out."

"No problem. I doubt anyone is watching to see how long your squad car has been parked out front."

Sam glared at him and stood. "Yeah, fine. I probably do have some things I need to get to this morning." He bent and kissed Mary Jo on the cheek. "Good to see you." He favored Eden with a besotted grin. "Welcome to Village Green. I hope to see you again, real soon."

Joe had to practically drag him from the house.

"What's your hurry, pretty boy?" Sam asked when they'd stepped through the front door and Joe closed it behind them.

"I wanted to get you out of there before you did something stupid. As it was, you were drooling all over that snappy uniform of yours. I was afraid you were about to cap it off by bending over and kissing her feet."

Sam appeared to give the idea some thought. "Tempting. She does have gorgeous feet. Gorgeous legs. Gorgeous body. Gorgeous face."

Joe started down the stairs. "Are cops allowed to ogle the citizenry?"

"Ogle?" Sam asked, matching his pace. "I was checking out the suspect."

"You certainly were. Very thoroughly."

"Yeah." Sam paused on the bottom step and sighed. "Based on my observations, I think we can safely assume she's not carrying any concealed weapons."

Joe snorted. "Like that took any brilliant police work. She's not wearing enough to conceal a matchbook. Maybe you should arrest her for indecency."

Sam headed down the brick path. "She wasn't indecent. Besides I would have thought you'd consider indecency a plus. Since when does a little nicely tanned skin bother you?"

"Since it's taken up residency at Mary Jo's."

Suddenly serious, Sam stopped. "You're not still worried about Eden are you? About her being trouble?"

Joe shoved his hands in his pockets and shrugged. "She's harmless."

Sam's expression lightened. "And you're not interested in her, right?"

"No way."

"So you don't mind if I—"

Joe smacked him on the shoulder before crossing to his truck parked at a weird angle in the driveway. "Have at it," he called. "But don't get too attached. She won't be staying long."

"Don't be such a pessimist. Maybe she'll change her mind."

After the men left, the residual testosterone fog was thick enough to cut with a knife. "Is that a regular occurrence?" Eden asked.

Mary Jo smiled wistfully. "It used to be. When the boys were growing up, it wasn't unusual to have Joe, Sam, and their friend Trey here for at least one meal a week. Matthew and I enjoyed it so much. It was like they were our boys. Of course, they've grown into men with their own busy lives now, so I don't see them as much anymore."

The sight of a uniformed policeman at the table took a bit of getting used to. Eden's experience with cops had been limited to the times one or two of them showed up at the door to haul off one of her mother's *Mr. Rights*. "Sam seems nice."

Mary Jo refilled her coffee cup and joined Eden at the table. "He's a doll, isn't he? He's always been so kind and thoughtful. Even as a teenager, Sam always looked for ways to help out."

"How did he get involved with someone like Joe? They seem like complete opposites."

"They *are* opposites, and yet the most loyal friends. Sam has stood by Joe all his life. His tender heart is always pulling for the underdog. I imagine that's why he became a policeman."

One word stood out to Eden. "Underdog? Joe?"

Mary Jo nodded. "It doesn't seem likely, does it? A big, strong man like him. He's not one anymore, certainly, but my Joseph had a rough childhood."

"What do you mean?"

"His mother left when he was about Jake's age, and his father was an abusive alcoholic."

Eden stroked a hand over Jake's curls. How could anyone walk out on a child? "Wow, that *is* rough. Poor Joe. So, how did he meet you and your husband?"

Mary Jo smiled. "God brought us together."

"Seems like God does that a lot. I mean, brings people to you."

Nice concept, not sure she totally understood or believed it. Mary Jo obviously did. "Jake and I are very grateful for your hospitality. You've been so nice to take us in and feed us and let us spend the night, but I think it's probably time we get on our way."

Mary Jo's mouth turned down in a pout. "You just got here. You can't leave so soon." Her expression brightened. "I have a wonderful idea. On Friday, I'm hosting the Ladies' Garden Club here at the house. It involves about twenty-five women who come for a tour and refreshments. The tour is no problem, but preparing a pretty spread for that many people is exhausting." She sent Eden a wheedling smile. "I wonder, would you be willing to stay and bake the goodies for me to serve?"

"I'm happy to bake anything you want, but Jake and I can't impose on you that long."

"It's no imposition. You'd be doing me a huge favor. And if you'll stay through the weekend, you'll have more opportunity to look over Village Green and see if it's the sort of place where you and Jake would like to live."

Eden chewed her lower lip. "It would be nice to get a feel for the town before we commit, but I don't want to be a burden to you."

Mary Jo batted the suggestion away with a swipe of her hand. "You two are the furthest thing from a burden. You're more like the fountain of youth. You've been here less than a day and already I feel ten years younger." Her face took on a serious expression. "I wouldn't be totally honest if I didn't admit that keeping you here is partially motivated by selfishness. I'm counting on your baking to drive the garden club wild with jealousy."

"Mary Jo!" Eden clapped a hand on her cheek in feigned shock.

"I know it's wicked." She grinned. "But I just can't help it. Eunice Welts and her apple cake with warm vanilla sauce have reigned as queen of desserts long enough."

"All right." Eden brought her fist down on the table with a decisive thump. "It's obvious we have to stay. And we'll unseat Eunice if it's the last thing we do." She removed Jake from the high chair and settled him on the floor to play with the stack of plastic containers Mary Jo had given him. "First thing, we need a plan. Have you got a sheet of paper and a pen? Let's come up with a menu, then I can strategize the prep times."

Mary Jo retrieved both from the built-in desk in the corner and handed them to Eden. "We'll need some of those blueberry muffins, of course."

"Sure." Eden wrote *muffins* on the top of the page. "Since it's a daytime event, let's make them mini muffins. They're cute and small, and your guests will be able to sample more things."

"That's a great idea." Mary Jo glanced toward the cabinet. "I think I have a couple of mini muffin pans."

"Do you mind checking to be certain? If I need to order supplies, I'll need to do it right away."

Mary Jo rooted through several spots before locating two aluminum mini muffin pans in the cabinet next to the sink. She held them high. "Muffin pans, check."

Eden grinned. "Perfect. So how do you feel about tarts?"

Her hostess's eyes lit. "I love them."

Eden added tarts to the list. "Me too. They're pretty and the tart shells can be made ahead of time."

Mary Jo smacked her lips. "What flavors can we have?"

"Let's do several and give the ladies some variety. Let's say chocolate, strawberry, and coconut cream."

"That sounds delicious." Mary Jo frowned. "I know I don't have individual tart pans."

"No problem. We'll put them on our list." Eden wrote tart pans in a separate column.

An hour later, they had a complete menu, a shopping list, and a cranky toddler.

Eden put down the pen. "I think I'll go upstairs and get Jake and I dressed. We need to head outside for a little exercise."

"Sounds good. The poor little man needs to run in the fresh air. If it's all right with you, I'll stay inside. I have a couple of things to take care of, and I'd better run a load of laundry."

"Of course, you can stay inside. We don't expect you to baby-sit us. In fact, since we're going to be here a week, let me extend a blanket invitation to you. You are always welcome to join us, but we know you're busy and have plenty to do. Please don't ever feel you have to entertain us."

"Perfect."

"I'd also like to help pay for groceries while we're here. Jake and I aren't freeloaders."

"Aren't you the dearest thing?" Mary Jo reached over to pat her hand. "It's so kind of you to offer, but I really can't accept. You're helping me with the party, and I'm providing room and board. That makes us even. Besides, Joe likes to supply at least half the food around here."

Somewhere during the planning, she'd forgotten about Joe. "He's not going to be too happy about our arrangement."

"Who, Joe?" Mary Jo waved a hand in breezy dismissal. "I'm sure he'll be delighted."

CHAPTER FOUR

Joe's gaze snapped up from the cutting board where he was slicing potatoes into thin discs. "You did *what*?"

Mary Jo pressed a finger to her lips. "Lower your voice, dear."

"They're out back. They can't hear me."

"When you roar like that, I imagine Sam can hear you all the way down at the police station." She smiled and calmly repeated, "I asked her to stay and help me with the Ladies' Garden Club meeting."

"What about the caterers you usually use?"

A swift look of guilt passed over her face. "I canceled them. I decided I wanted something more personal this year."

He narrowed his eyes. "You just wanted to keep the blonde and her kid here."

She lifted her chin. "Yes, I did."

He finished cutting the last potato and placed the knife on the counter. "This is crazy. You do not need to be taking in boarders."

"Oh no, dear, they're not boarders. That would mean I was collecting rent from them. I would never do such a thing. Eden offered to pay me when I asked them to stay a few days." She moved closer and lowered her voice to a whisper. "Poor child. I get the impression she's had to scrape for everything. She's very independent. And a bit sensitive about taking what she perceives as charity."

He didn't want to think of her as a poor child. He preferred to consider her a scheming opportunist. "She seems resilient enough."

"She reminds me of you when you were young."

He snorted. "She's not *that* bad."

Mary Jo giggled at the face he made. "You were an absolute delight. Such a bright little boy, so affectionate and eager to please. Matthew always said he couldn't ask for a better son."

"I bet he said that to me a hundred times." Joe picked up a handful of potato slices and arranged them in a neat row in the bottom of a casserole pan. He remembered so clearly the very first time Matthew said it. Joe had been a skittish kid. He'd been backhanded by his father enough that he was never too sure when the next blow was coming. To make himself less of a target, he'd made the conscious decision to keep at least an arm's length away from adults at all times. Just to be safe.

The summer Joe turned eleven, Matthew surprised him. He closed the distance between them before Joe could move away and rested his big hands on Joe's shoulders. Joe reared back, flailing like an animal caught in a trap. Matthew held him, gently but firmly, and waited until Joe's furtively darting eyes came to rest on his. Once he'd gained Joe's full attention, he crouched down until their faces were on the same level and only inches apart. The look on the older man's face had been so kind and full of understanding that Joe knew he didn't have to be afraid.

Their eyes had held while Matthew said, "I want you to know what a treasure you are. You are a fine young man, and if I'd been blessed with a son of my own, I would want him to be just like you."

Joe's mouth had gone slack. Matthew was a man of integrity. If he said something, then it was true. If he said Joe was a treasure and just the thing he would want in a son, then Joe could believe it.

Those words marked a turning point in Joe's life.

His circumstances didn't change. He still lived in a shack at the edge of town with a drunken bully for a father. Kids at school still made fun of him.

But Joe changed. From that day forward, he didn't hear the insults from his father or the mocking of his peers. He was a treasure, a fine young man, and the son Matthew wanted.

And he determined he would live his life in such a way that he would never let Matthew down.

Joe finished laying out the last row of potatoes. "I miss Matthew." He picked up the pan of cheese sauce simmering on the stove and poured it over the top.

Mary Jo nodded. "I do too. I'm sorry he's not here to meet Eden and Jake. Wouldn't he just love them?"

He probably would. Matthew had had a tender heart the size of Texas. But he wasn't here, so it was up to Joe to step in and protect Mary Jo.

"I don't want you to get too attached to them." He carried the casserole to the oven and slid it in. "I have a feeling once the week is over, they'll be moving on."

Mary Jo's face fell. "Why do you say that? Village Green is a wonderful town. It would be the perfect place to raise a family."

He met her gaze. "I just think we need to be realistic. There's nothing here to keep them. First off, she'll need to find work to support her and the kid. I'm not aware of a single full-time job open in town. If she was fortunate enough to find work, she'd have to find inexpensive housing."

Her smile was back in full force. "That's easy. I have plenty of space. They can live here with me."

He shook his head. "She'd never do it. You said it yourself, she wouldn't accept charity."

Mary Jo's lips compressed into a determined line. "There must be some way to keep her here."

Joe laughed. "Do you know, I'm actually afraid when I see the wheels turning in your head? I think you need to stop scheming and resign yourself to enjoying their company for the week and then seeing them off."

The terrace door opened and closed.

Mary Jo called, "We're in here."

Eden walked in with the kid in her arms and stopped in the doorway. Her smile faded when she saw him. "Oh. You're here."

He spread his arms wide. "Tuesday night. Dinner with Joe." Despite his best intentions to ignore her, his gaze traveled from her head to her toes. Even in a T-shirt streaked with dirt and her long blonde hair caught up in a messy bun, she was stunning. To demonstrate he was completely unaffected by her, he focused a look of disdain on her feet. "What's the deal with you and bare feet? Don't Florida girls wear shoes?"

She wiggled her tanned toes defiantly. "Not if we can help it. What's the deal with you and rude personal remarks? Don't Texas boys have any manners?"

"Really, Joseph." Mary Jo tsked. "What must Eden think of you?"

"Don't worry, Mary Jo. I don't think of him at all." She sent him a satisfied smirk, clearly pleased for having had the last word. "I came in to ask if there was time to clean up before dinner."

He glanced at the clock hanging over the sink. "Dinner will be ready in about an hour."

"That's plenty of time. Did Mary Jo tell you there are yeast rolls in the fridge?"

"Oh, mercy, I completely forgot." Mary Jo hurried to the refrigerator and pulled out a cookie sheet dotted with dough balls. "Eden made homemade rolls for us."

If they were anything like her blueberry muffins, they'd be amazing, not that he'd ever admit it to her. "Okay. How long do they need to bake?"

"Fifteen minutes," Eden said. "At 350."

Joe took the rolls from Mary Jo. "Got it."

Eden turned to her son. "All right, Mister Jake. Time for you and me to find something clean to wear. We'll see you all in a bit."

"Bit," Jake confirmed with a nod while she whisked him away.

An hour later, Joe joined the women and Jake at the table, the four of them holding hands while Mary Jo prayed. Since the others had their eyes closed, Joe took a moment to study Eden's hand. Her fingers were long and slender, her nails softly rounded and unpainted. A capable hand, strong and yet unmistakably feminine. She snatched it away as soon as Mary Jo said amen.

"Why don't I serve the potatoes, since they just came out of the oven?" He picked up Eden's plate and scooped a double portion, then returned it to the table in front of her. "Let them cool for a moment before you give them to Jake." He frowned. Why was he advising her how to feed the kid?

Instead of giving him a smart answer like he expected or deserved, she flashed him a full-on smile. Whoa. His heart actually skipped a beat.

"It all looks delicious, Joe." Mary Jo took a pork chop and passed the platter to Eden.

Eden took a serving and handed the dish to him. "It smells great. So, where did you learn to cook like this?"

He nodded toward their hostess. "Mary Jo taught me everything I know."

Eden's brows shot up. "Really?" She turned to Mary Jo. "I thought you didn't cook."

"It's not that I can't cook." Mary Jo served herself some peas and passed the bowl to Eden. "I just don't. Too much bother for only myself." She smiled. "Now if you and Jake lived here, I would be happy to do the cooking."

Eden laughed and shook her head. "I think after having us under your roof for a week, you'll be glad enough to see us go."

"What will you do?" Joe interrupted before Mary Jo offered to file a petition to adopt them and move them in permanently. "What are your plans?"

Eden spooned a mound of peas onto Jake's tray and gave the bowl to Joe. "Up in the air right now. Jake and I will take some time over the next few days to look around Village Green and see if it would be a good fit for us. If so, I'd need to find a job and an apartment, and day care for my little guy."

He nodded. "What kind of job are you looking for?"

"My first choice would be a bakery since that's where I have work experience."

"You certainly have a gift. These rolls are delicious." Mary Jo spread butter on the remaining half. "How did you get started baking? I bet you're one of those people who has always loved tinkering around in the kitchen."

Eden shook her head. "I took it up for purely practical reasons. I needed a job after Jake was a couple of months old, and the local bakery had an eleven to seven shift."

"You worked the night shift?" Mary Jo's question ended in a squeak.

"Yep. Since we were living with my mom, I could put Jake down to sleep and be home before he woke up. If he did happen to wake up during the night, she was okay with giving him a bottle and putting him back to bed. Luckily, he's a great sleeper."

Joe didn't want to be interested. This woman was not his problem, but the question popped out before he could stop it. "When did *you* sleep?"

"During Jake's naps and a couple hours before I went in to work."

He grimaced. "Sounds brutal. You must have been sleep-deprived."

She shrugged while scooping another serving of peas onto Jake's tray. "It was okay. And it saved me the expense of day care. Now that he's older and we're not living with my mom, I would need to work the day shift." She turned to Mary Jo. "Does Village Green have a bakery?"

Mary Jo lowered her fork. "No, dear."

"The closest bakery is thirty minutes away in Corsicana," Joe said.

"Oh. Does the grocery store I saw on Main Street have an in-house bakery?"

He'd never noticed. His eyes met Mary Jo's in an unspoken question. When she shrugged, he turned to Eden. "Not that I'm aware of."

Eden frowned. "Well, I can check on it. If not, I could get a job at a day care. They typically don't pay very well, but they might let me keep Jake there for free."

"That's a possibility." Even upbeat Mary Jo didn't sound hopeful. "What other things could you do?"

"I guess I could waitress."

Mary Jo bobbed her head. "We do have a restaurant in town."

With her looks, she'd collect a fortune in tips. Joe sliced off the last bite of his pork chop and popped it in his mouth. Unfortunately, Estelle's was the one restaurant in town, and she only employed a couple of part-timers to cover rushes.

"I'm open to doing pretty much anything." Eden lifted her chin and raw determination shone in her eyes. "I'm a hard worker and pick things up quickly. Unfortunately, I don't have my college degree since I dropped out my junior year after Jake was born." Her expression softened to a smile when she looked at her son. "But it's all good because I have this great little man, and we are family."

Mary Jo beamed at her. "You are a wonderful family, and I believe the Lord will open up something for you."

It was news to Joe that God ran an employment agency, but from experience, he knew when Mary Jo and her Lord got involved, anything could happen. Whatever, he was ready to change the subject. The idea of the blonde and her kid living hand-to-mouth was too close to his own blighted childhood. He wouldn't wish that on anyone.

"Mary Jo says you're going to help her with the garden club thing on Friday."

She'd just taken a bite and nodded.

"We've come up with a wonderful menu," Mary Jo said. "If it's not too warm, we're going to serve everything on the terrace, which means we'll have to move a lot of furniture. Would you be available to help us set up tables and chairs?"

He considered her guileless blue eyes. What was Mary Jo up to? He'd seen her knock out a party for a hundred without breaking a sweat. Suddenly she was calling on him for backup? Of course, previously she'd had a caterer to do the heavy lifting. Maybe she'd discovered she'd taken on more than she and Miss Florida could handle. "Sure. When do you need me?"

The satisfied smile she sent him said he'd fallen into her plan, whatever it was. "Why don't you count on being here all day?"

Since her arrival, Eden and Mary Jo took turns preparing breakfast. They hadn't made a formal schedule; everything just fell into place. Whoever was up first made a pot of coffee and something for everyone to eat. Today Eden fixed scrambled eggs and toast.

She and Mary Jo had finished eating, but since Jake seemed content smearing the remains of his meal around on his tray, Eden indulged in the luxury of lingering over coffee.

"Jake and I are going to go to the grocery store this morning to get supplies for Friday."

Mary Jo met her gaze over her mug and smiled. "Let me know what time you want to go, and I can drive you."

"Thank you, but unless you just want to get out of the house, it's not necessary. I remember where the store is. We passed it when we drove into town. I know you have lots to do to get ready, and there is no reason for us both to go."

Mary Jo seemed to weigh her options for a moment. "I should probably stay home if you're certain you're okay going by yourself. I can use the time to prepare my little welcome speech for the ladies. I don't know why I dread it so much." She hopped up from the table. "Let me get you some money, and you can leave whenever you're ready."

"Oh no, I don't need any money. I've got this." She'd taken a hard look at their finances last night after she'd put Jake down. She could spare some of the funds she'd put away for their new beginning without endangering their future, and she wanted to do something to repay Mary Jo for everything she'd done.

Her hostess disappeared for a moment and returned with a hot pink handbag. She pulled bills from her wallet, laid them next to Eden's plate, and smiled. "Your job is to bake, not to furnish the refreshments."

"But I'd like to." Eden held Mary Jo's gaze. "Please."

Mary Jo rested a hand on her shoulder. "You are the sweetest thing, but I really can't accept it. You see, I don't think I would be officially beating Eunice Welts if I didn't at least pay for the winning dessert."

Eden arched a brow. "Are you saying there are rules for one-upmanship?"

"Oh, absolutely." Mary Jo said it with a perfectly straight face. "One would hate to stray into bad sportsmanship."

Eden laughed and shook her head. "There is no one like you."

Mary Jo's blue eyes twinkled. "Joe tells me the same thing all the time. I'm not entirely certain he means it as a compliment."

He might be a jerk, but he adored Mary Jo. "I'm sure he does. Even a jer—er, a guy like him can see you are an incredibly generous person."

Mary Jo's face lit up. "You've just paid me the highest compliment. I want to be generous because God has been so generous with me. Imagine the Creator of the universe inviting us to become His children."

"Wait." Eden focused her full attention on Mary Jo. "Aren't we *all* God's children?" She thought she remembered that bit of theology from a popular Christmas song.

"We are all God's *creation*," Mary Jo said. "We have to *choose* to become His child."

Eden frowned. "How do you know that?"

"It's in the Bible." Mary Jo smiled. "I know from reading the Bible that God loves us and wants us to be in His family."

Family. Something deep inside Eden had been looking for a place to belong since she was a little girl.

The only child of a single mother, she and her mom were technically a family, but in reality, they were not. Her mother loved her, but the focus of her life had always been on finding the perfect man to complete her. Somewhere in the endless succession of potential mates, Eden had been pushed to the side. She'd never been neglected, just relegated to a lesser status.

When Eden got to college and met Jake's father, she thought she'd found someone to belong to, the nucleus for her own family. Mark Siegler was everything her mother's men were not—smart, hardworking, focused on making something of himself. Mark wanted to be a doctor. The fact he came from a large, close-knit family was a definite plus.

Looking back, she realized she'd woven a fairy-tale future for the two of them over the year and a half they dated. When their relationship progressed to physical intimacy, she'd given herself wholeheartedly. After all, theirs was a forever love.

Then he was accepted to medical school, and everything changed.

Suddenly, his bright future didn't include her. He'd be going off to school, then doing a minimum of four years in residency. She could tag along, he'd said, but really he didn't see having any time or energy for her. Even his family agreed she'd only be a hindrance. A trap.

Her fairy tale unraveled. They broke up. Her heart was broken.

And she was pregnant.

He'd already headed off to a school on the west coast when the drug store test confirmed it. She didn't tell him about the baby. By then, nothing remained between them. And if the idea of a girlfriend was a hindrance and a trap, she hated to think what he'd say about a baby.

Jake pushed his sippy cup off the tray, and Eden bent to retrieve it. He grinned when she returned it to him and immediately pushed it off again. One of his favorite games.

"Doesn't it seem like if God"—she replaced Jake's cup, then lifted her arms and spread them wide to signify the immenseness of such a being—"wanted us to be His family, He could just 'poof' us all into His children?"

Mary Jo grinned. "That would certainly be easier, but He has given us free will to make our own decisions. He wants us to choose Him."

"I've never heard any of this." Eden caught Jake's cup in mid-fall and handed it back to him. "Honestly, the few times I've thought about God, I imagined Him to be a mean old man in a long white robe looking for ways to punish me."

Mary Jo nodded. "I think that's a pretty common misconception. Probably because He looks like that in all the cartoons. Jesus gave us a more accurate picture when He told His followers that they should think of God as their heavenly Father."

Eden frowned. "I haven't had much luck with fathers. My mother got pregnant right out of high school, and the guy took off. And Jake's father was gone before I knew I was pregnant." The shameful truths that usually stuck in her throat rolled easily off her tongue. How wonderful to unburden herself to someone who listened and didn't judge.

Mary Jo's gentle smile never wavered. "People who have had bad experiences with their earthly fathers sometimes have difficulty believing in an all-loving, gracious Father. The biggest hurdle you'll have to clear is to know that God will never leave you. He promises never to leave or forsake His children. The Bible also says you are so important to Him that He even knows the number of hairs on your head."

Eden absently reached for her braid. This all sounded too good to be true. Eden Lambert from Tallahassee who had pretty much messed up her whole life and never gave God more than a passing thought was important to Him? "Really?"

Mary Jo's smile widened and she nodded.

Something warm stirred inside Eden. God loved her and wanted her in His family? She wouldn't believe it on the word of one person, even someone as nice as Mary Jo. A claim like that was too important to get wrong. She'd have to look into it, to see for herself what the Bible had to say. And if it was true . . . well, clearly her life would never be the same.

While they talked, Jake's play with the sippy cup had progressed from pushing it off the edge of his tray to throwing it. Time to give him some attention.

"I'm not done with our discussion, but apparently Jake is." Eden stood and carried her dishes to the sink. "I'm going to take him upstairs and get changed. Once we get cleaned up, we'll head off to the grocery store."

"We can talk later," Mary Jo said. "While you two are gone, I will force myself to sit here until I've written my little speech."

Eden parked in the small lot behind the Grocery Giant. She unfastened Jake from his car seat and carried him inside. Since they didn't provide a sanitizing wipe dispenser in the cart area, she pulled one from the packet in her purse and wiped down the seat, sides, and handle. Although Jake had thankfully outgrown the habit of slumping over and sucking on any accessible part of the grocery cart, she knew his little fingers would be everywhere and then into his mouth.

She eased him off her hip and into the seat, connecting the belt around his waist with a click.

"Cook-ee?" he asked with a wide grin. "Cook-ee?"

"We'll see." At the grocery store back home, the ladies in the bakery always had a free cookie for the kids—Jake's favorite part of the trip. "I don't know if they have cookies here."

Grocery Giant was small by Tallahassee standards. Unlike the shiny new superstores at home, this store offered limited natural light, lower ceilings, and narrow aisles. If she chose to settle here, this was the only place to shop. Happily, though cramped, Grocery Giant smelled clean and looked tidy. She could make it work.

The store appeared to be laid out in the reverse of the one she shopped in Tallahassee. A small deli counter was the first department on her right. Across the aisle from the deli were shelves of commercially packaged bread and rolls. If they had an in-house bakery, this would be the logical location.

She approached the older man in a white paper hat behind the counter. "Hi. I'm new in the area, and I wondered if you have an in-house bakery here?"

He smiled. "No, ma'am. But we have every kind of bread and roll and tortilla on those shelves right there." He pointed across the aisle. "Is there anything special you're looking for?"

"Do you carry cakes or pastries?"

He bobbed his head. "Yes, ma'am. We have several nice varieties in the freezer section along the far wall. I'm particular to the Sara Lee chocolate layer cakes, myself. You just leave them out on the counter to thaw for a couple of hours and they're ready to go."

She kept her expression neutral while her hopes took a dive. Frozen cakes were not a good sign. "Okay. Thank you."

"Did you say you've moved in?"

Eden shook her head. "No, we're just visiting right now."

"Well, welcome. Village Green is a fine place to live."

Not if I can't find a job. "Thank you." She waved as she and Jake moved away.

Of course, just because there was no bakery in town didn't mean she couldn't find work. But this morning's short trip had opened her eyes to just how small Village Green was. Driving into town the other day, she'd let the quaint park benches and flower-pots distract her. Today, she'd looked past the trimmings to the possible opportunities. A restaurant, a pharmacy/gift shop, a bank, a hardware store, and a grocery store. That's it. Not a lot of potential for employment.

Eden guided the cart to the baking aisle. Experience told her she had about thirty minutes before Jake lost patience. A tired, cookie-less toddler in the grocery store was a recipe for disaster.

She marked the items off her list when she dropped them into the basket. Flour, check. No fancy brands here. A couple of bags of white sugar, check. Ditto for brown sugar, check. Four tiny bottles of vanilla extract, check, check, check, check. Thankfully the store carried a decent brand of cocoa powder and the coconut she needed for the tarts, check, check.

She and Jake were making good time as she rolled over to the dairy case and loaded up on butter, cream, half-and-half, and eggs. Done. Mary Jo would be picking up the produce they needed tomorrow.

She guided the cart to the registers at the front of the store. Only one of the three was open, and no one was ahead of her, so she pulled in and greeted the cashier.

The woman, wearing the most astonishing shimmery blue eye shadow, gave her a long, measuring look. "You must be new here."

Eden tried not to stare at the dazzling stripes of blue. "I'm just visiting."

The woman looked pointedly at the contents of the cart. "Must be doing a lot of baking on your visit."

"My hostess is having a party."

"Who are you staying with?"

Her first reaction was to tell her to mind her own business. However, this was a small town, and it wouldn't be smart to make enemies if she and Jake were going to settle here. Truthfully, everyone she'd met, with the exception of Joe, had been super warm and friendly. Maybe this interrogation was just the local's way of getting to know her.

"Mary Jo Piermont."

"Oh, yeah. She throws parties all the time." She reached into the basket. "She's really great."

"Yes, she is." Eden opened her handbag and focused rapt attention there, hoping to put an end to the cross-examination.

The clerk busied herself running items over the scanner, bagging them, and placing the filled bags at the end of her counter. Overhead, George Strait crooned about lost love.

The respite was short-lived. "So, how long are you staying?"

Eden lifted her head from her purse. "Just a few days."

Jake had been watching expectantly while she dug through her bag. When nothing was forthcoming, he said plaintively, "Treat. Treat."

"Cute kid. He yours?"

"Yes, he is. Thank you." Eden dove back into her bag, rooting around for a snack to appease Jake. She found a dog-eared bag of fruit snacks at the bottom.

"Treat." His voice became shrill, the sure promise of an impending meltdown.

"Yes, honey. Right here." She tore open the packet and handed him two. "Treat."

He examined them, smiled broadly, and popped them into his mouth.

"How old is he?"

"Eighteen months." Eden glanced at the cart. Nearly empty. They were in the home stretch now.

"I don't see a ring. You married?"

"No, I'm not." Eden tamped down her rising irritation. A few more minutes of this and she and Jake would *both* blow sky high.

"That'll be $127.53."

Eden pulled out the bills Mary Jo had given her, peeled off seven twenties, and handed them to her.

The clerk bent over the register drawer to make Eden's change. After collecting the bills and coins, she straightened and counted them into Eden's hand.

Jake was done. He refused the next round of fruit snacks she offered and began to howl.

"He really is a beautiful little boy." The woman raised her voice to be heard over the noise. "His father must have been a real looker, huh?"

Eden was done, too, as embarrassed by the relentless grilling as she was by Jake's high-pitched wailing. Small town or not, she was finished supplying answers to the prying questions. She offered the woman a vague shrug in response to her latest question and stuffed the change into her purse, pushed the cart forward, and hurriedly loaded it with the bags.

"I should have introduced myself. I'm Marilyn Bray."

Eden tossed the last bag into the cart. Aware that she couldn't afford to be rude, but knowing she was all out of nice, she managed a curt nod. "Eden Lambert."

She kept her shoulders back and head high while she calmly wheeled the loaded cart and shrieking child from the store.

The automatic door had just swished closed behind her when Sam pulled up in his patrol car. He lowered the window. "Hey, Eden." He frowned. "What's the matter with Jake?"

"Grocery store meltdown. We exceeded our thirty-minute limit. He'll be fine once I get him home."

Sam glanced toward the lot. "Where are you parked? Let me help you get the groceries into your car, and I can follow you to Mary Jo's and carry them inside for you."

"I can't ask you to do that."

"You didn't ask. I offered." He smiled.

She sighed. "Thank you. I could really use the help. If you're sure it's okay? Looks to me like you're on duty."

"Absolutely. My duty is to serve and protect."

CHAPTER FIVE

Friday morning, Joe let himself into Mary Jo's house a little before seven. He moved soundlessly on sneakered feet to the kitchen, intent upon completing the food prep Mary Jo had assigned to him before everyone was awake.

He was surprised to find the kitchen lights on and Eden standing at the counter with her back to him, busy at work over a tray of something. "What are you doing up so early?"

She jolted and dropped her spoon with a clatter. Hand over her heart, she whirled around to glare at him. "You just scared me half to death."

And enjoyed it. He continued closer to peer over her shoulder. "What are you doing?"

She returned her attention to her work. "I'm stealing the family silver. What does it look like?"

He laughed. "It looks like you're making hundreds of tiny little pies." His gaze made a leisurely trip from her busy fingers, up her tanned arms, and came to rest on her tank top and shorts. Suddenly he didn't feel like smiling anymore. "Don't you have a robe?"

"It's dozens. They're tarts. And no." She was a study in continuous motion. She rinsed the dropped spoon at the sink and returned to the tray of pastries where she spooned some sort of pudding into each shell. "Had I known you were coming before dawn, I would have dressed for company."

"Are those the crusts you were baking last night?"

Scoop. Plop. Scoop. Plop. She nodded, never looking up, never losing her rhythm. "They need to be filled so they can chill for four hours. I thought I'd do them while Jake was still sleeping."

Joe glanced at the baby monitor she'd placed at the edge of her workspace. "Uh-oh. Little dude is stirring."

She nodded. "He's been awake for about fifteen minutes. I figure I've got another five before I have to get him."

"Do you need help?"

That got her attention. She lowered her spoon and turned to face him with raised brows. "Did I just hear you right? Did you offer to *help*?" She tilted her head and narrowed her eyes. "Are you being nice to me?"

"Maybe." He gave her a bland look and a shrug. "Don't get used to it."

"I won't. Okay, wash your hands and you can put the strawberry halves on the tarts."

He soaped, rinsed at the sink, and dried his hands on the dish towel on the counter. "You better do one first. I need an example so I don't mess up."

She retrieved a bowl of cut strawberries from the refrigerator, set it on the kitchen table, carried over the tray of tarts she'd filled, and placed it beside the bowl. "Okay, we're going to fit four halves on each tart." She gently laid berries on the custard to form a sort of a flower.

"Cool. When did you wash and cut all these?"

She picked more strawberries from the bowl and placed them on the next tart. "This morning."

Joe frowned. "What time did you get up?"

"About five." Efficient as a machine, her nimble fingers continued to form berry flowers.

He gave a low whistle. "I know you didn't get to bed until after midnight because you were still up when I left, so you got, what, four hours of sleep?"

"I guess."

He scooped up a handful of fruit and laid them out just as she had. Nothing to it. "You're nuts. You're going to be wiped out before the party even starts."

"No, I've got it." Her quiet voice rang with the confident determination he was coming to associate with her. "I'll probably crash after I put Jake down tonight, but it'll be worth it. I want Mary Jo's party to be amazing."

He snorted. "I don't know about amazing. I mean, it's just a bunch of old ladies wandering around in the backyard, but the food will be outstanding."

Eden stopped and slowly turned to face him. "Did I just hear a compliment?"

He could feel the heat of her gaze, but to give her back some of her own, he didn't look up from his task. "Looks like. Don't get excited. I don't have to like you to know you're a wizard with an oven. I figure I'll butter you up a bit, so you'll let me have one of these little babies."

"Whew. A glimpse of your bad-tempered self. For a minute there I was afraid you were sick." She returned to the counter. "I made extra strawberry tarts so there ought to be leftovers. But you don't get them until the party is over and the last guest is gone."

Happy little chirps came across the monitor. "Time's up. I'll get Jake, then I'll be back in a minute."

"Take your time." He fitted another strawberry flower onto a tart. "I have plenty to keep me busy."

He manfully resisted the temptation to watch her exit, to follow the progress of the micro shorts and tank top. He listened to her light tread on the stairs, then heard her voice on the monitor when she joined her son.

The kid was so excited to see her that he belly-laughed his delight. The full, joyous sound brought a smile to Joe's face. He didn't have to have children to recognize that little boy was special, and the bond between him and his mom was priceless.

He glanced up when they arrived in the kitchen, relieved yet disappointed she'd added the men's shirt over her previous outfit.

"This is my last one." He pointed to the tart. "Do you want me to put the tray back in the refrigerator?"

"I need to glaze them first." She sat Jake in his high chair and snapped the tray over him. "Can you say good morning to Joe?"

"Joe," he said with a toothy smile. His gaze traveled to the bowl of fruit. He pointed and said something unrecognizable that clearly meant "hand over the strawberries."

"Can I give him a few?" Joe looked to Eden for permission. "Are we done with these?"

"Yes, but they need to be cut into smaller pieces so he doesn't choke." She fished a paring knife out of the drawer and walked it to the table.

"I've got this." Joe lifted the knife from her hand. He sat in the chair next to Jake and frowned up at her skeptical expression. "What? You don't think I can cut strawberries?"

She said nothing but lingered to watch as he plucked one from the bowl, neatly carved it into four segments, and placed them on Jake's tray. The kid grinned and stuffed two of the pieces in his mouth. He repeated the same unintelligible word from a minute ago.

She smiled. "You do realize you are now his slave. He won't let up until they're all gone."

"No problem. I've got plenty of time." He cut another berry and put it on the tray. Jake ate them as fast as they appeared. "You go ahead and do what you need to do."

She carried the decorated pastries over to the counter. "Why are you here so early?" She looked up from spooning something over them. "I thought you'd set up all the tables and chairs last night."

"I did. But since I'd already committed to being here, I asked if there was anything else I could do. Mary Jo assigned me the fruit and vegetable trays."

Eden nodded. "So, *you* help her with parties. I wondered how one woman accomplished all this."

He could tell her about the army of caterers Mary Jo kept on speed dial, the team of experts she regularly called in to prepare and serve her lavish parties, but he didn't. Mary Jo had her reasons, and he wouldn't get in her way. "Uh-oh. Running out of strawberries. What's next?"

"I'll get him a yogurt. You've done your time. You need to get started on the fruit and vegetables." She caught his eye when he stood. "Thank you."

"Tank you," Jake parroted.

Joe reached over and patted the almost white halo of curls. "You're welcome, little man. Anytime." He wouldn't want one of his own, but this kid was really cute.

"Good morning, everyone." Mary Jo sailed into the kitchen, full of energy and wearing her trademark ear-to-ear smile.

Jake banged his tray. "May Jo, May Jo."

"Good morning, Master Jake." She walked over to the high chair to plant a smacking kiss on top of his head, straightened, and surveyed the room. "It looks like you all have been busy this morning."

Joe tilted his head toward Eden. "Your baker has been up since five."

Her smile dimmed. "Mercy, Eden! You must be exhausted."

Eden waved off the concern. "Not at all. I wanted to get the majority of things finished before Jake got up. I plan to set everything out when he goes down for a nap."

Mary Jo caught sight of the tray Eden was working on. "Those strawberry tarts are beautiful."

"She made extra and promised I can have the leftovers." Joe scrubbed carrots under the stream from the faucet. "If you play your cards right, I'll share one with you."

"The coconut tarts are finished," Eden called over her shoulder. "If you want to see them, they're in the refrigerator. The chocolate ones are in there, too, but they won't be done until I top them off with whipped cream and chocolate shavings, right before we put them out."

Mary Jo opened the refrigerator door for a peek. "It all looks so delicious."

"I'm about to mix up the blueberry muffins." Eden pointed to the ingredients she'd lined up on the counter. "They're the last thing I have to bake."

Aw man, the amazing muffins. Joe's mouth watered. "I hope you're making extras."

Eden nodded. "Yes, and I won't make you wait for leftovers. As payment for your help this morning, you get some straight out of the oven."

"He helped you?" Mary Jo's eyes went wide, and she stared up at him. "You helped her?"

"Disturbing, isn't it?" Eden grinned and lifted her shoulders in an exaggerated shrug. "He's been nice to me all morning."

Mary Jo frowned. "That does seem out of character for him."

He waved a hand. "Hello? I'm right here."

"Yes, you are, dear one." Mary Jo captured his face in her hands. "And we are so glad." She looked around. "Everybody is so busy. What can *I* do to help?"

Joe pointed to the table. "You can sit down and have a cup of coffee."

She ignored his suggestion. "I can help you wash the fruit and vegetables."

"I've got it." He set down the carrots and dried his hands before gently shepherding her to the table. "Sit down. You need to save your strength for the big party."

Eden looked up from stirring. "Do you have to give a tour?"

Mary Jo shook her head. "Not really. These women have been here dozens of times. They know their way around the gardens as well as I do."

He delivered a cup of coffee to her. "The Ladies' Garden Club is just an excuse to gather and eat party food and gossip, isn't that right?"

Mary Jo giggled. "That's not what it says in the club charter, but it's probably a pretty accurate assessment. Not the part about gossip. These ladies are too nice for that."

Joe knew better. "Correction. Mary Jo is too nice to know when other people aren't."

After lunch, Eden put Jake down for his nap and hurried to her room to get dressed. She wasn't an invited guest, but she wanted to wear something that reflected well on her hostess.

She opened the closet where her one dress, a white cotton sundress that had seen at least a dozen washings, hung in solitary splendor. She stripped out of her shorts and T-shirt, pulled the dress over her head, and stepped into the bathroom to get a look in the full-length mirror. The dress wasn't fancy, but it was miles up from the shorts and jeans that made up the bulk of her meager wardrobe. She smoothed her hands down her sides and took one more critical look. Not great, but it would have to do.

She swept her hair up into an easy bun and secured it with a couple of pins. She brushed her teeth and added a touch of rosy gloss to her lips. One last look in the mirror and she headed out.

Mary Jo met her at the foot of the stairs. "Oh, Eden," she said, capturing her hands, "you look lovely. Stunning."

Eden felt her face heat. "I just hope I don't embarrass you in front of your friends."

Mary Jo's expression became serious. She locked gazes with Eden. "I will never be embarrassed by you. You are a treasure and a delight."

Joe walked out of the kitchen. "You're going to want to let loose of the *treasure and delight* so she can get to work, or the old ladies are going to arrive before we get the food out."

Mary Jo winked at Eden before releasing her to look at her watch. "It's almost time, isn't it? I guess I better get upstairs and change."

Eden followed Joe into the kitchen. Two large round silver trays waited on the table, one laid out with fruit, the other with vegetables. "Did you do that? Arrange it, I mean?"

He nodded.

"It's beautiful. Really nice." She studied him from beneath furrowed brows. "You are clearly a man of hidden depths."

"Was that a compliment?" he asked. "Because it sounded like one to me."

She laughed. "In your dreams." She glanced at the clock over the sink. "I guess it's time to put the food out."

"I'll do it," Joe said. "You need to finish up the tarts."

Eden went to the refrigerator and collected the bowl of whipped cream she'd made while Jake sat captive in the high chair during lunch. She pulled out the tray of chocolate tarts and set it on the counter. Her gaze bounced from the whipped cream to the tarts. To pipe or to spoon?

She experimented by spooning a dollop of cream into the center of the chocolate custard, then sprinkling it with chocolate shavings.

"What do you think?" she asked Joe when he reentered the kitchen to get the other tray.

He stopped behind her left shoulder. "If you are asking if I'd like to eat one, the answer is yes."

She leaned into him, driving an elbow into his ribs. "I'm asking if they look pretty enough to serve this way, or do I need to pipe the whipped cream?"

"They look great like that. I hope you made extras."

"I did. Of course, everything depends on how hungry the ladies are."

"We'll encourage them to fill up on vegetables." He reached across her, snitched a couple of chocolate shavings, and walked away.

The spooned dollop method went quickly, and Eden had the tray finished in no time. She carried it to the dining room and rested it on the corner of the table.

Originally, they'd talked about serving the food outdoors, but when the weatherman predicted high eighties for the day, they changed their plans. Even in the shade, the food would quickly spoil.

They'd moved the chairs from around the massive mahogany table to the perimeter of the high-ceilinged room, so the ladies had a place to sit and easy access to the goodies. Mary Jo had covered the table with two cloths. The first, a springy shade of green, peeked through the second, a length of antique ecru lace. She'd arranged an enormous centerpiece of pink and white blooms cut from the garden and placed it beneath the sparkling chandelier.

The effect was so elegant, so beautiful, it looked like a layout in a high-end ladies' magazine.

Eden had helped Mary Jo set out serving pieces, some tiered, others heavily chased silver trays from an impressive collection she stored in a vault-like closet in the hall. Joe had used the two big round ones for the fruit and vegetables and had already placed the completed trays on either side of the table. Eden put chocolate tarts on the bottom level of each of the three-tiered servers. Once they were arranged to her satisfaction, she filled in the other two tiers with the strawberry and coconut tarts.

Next came the plates of muffins, brownies, and salted caramel bars. Finally, she set out a platter of the iced sugar cookies she'd painstakingly decorated to look like flowers.

Mary Jo was waiting for her when she returned to the kitchen. She corralled Joe with one arm and Eden with the other into a perfumed group hug. "I want to thank you two for all your hard work. Everything looks lovely. Really, it looks more professional than anything the finest caterers have done. We are going to be the talk of the club."

Eden cocked up her chin and grinned. "All I can say is Eunice Welts better watch her back."

Mary Jo chuckled at their little joke. "I wish you would both come to the party. It would be more fun."

Joe stepped out of her hold and shook his head. "You know I love you, but no way on earth I'm hanging out with the garden club. I'll stick around long enough to replenish ice and drinks at the stations outside, then I'm outta here."

Eden glanced toward the baby monitor on the counter. "I've probably only got an hour before Jake wakes up. I'll keep the food refilled until then. After his nap, we'll go for a walk to keep him out of the way until the party is over."

Mary Jo pushed out her bottom lip. "I don't know why you won't stay and let me show you off." A knock sounded on the front door, and she hurried away to answer it.

By two fifteen the house was filled with chatter and laughter. Joe closed the swinging door leading into the kitchen. "That should hold them off."

Eden laughed. "I can't believe that you, of all people, are intimidated by a bunch of old women. I thought you were the big ladies' man."

"Those aren't ladies." He nodded toward the door. "They're wolves, traveling in packs and searching for fresh kill."

The door swung open, and Mary Jo popped her head in. "Eden, you've just got to come out here so I can introduce you. Everyone wants to meet the young lady behind the food."

Eden glanced at Joe and gestured for him to join her. He shook his head. "Not a chance. I've met them before. The spotlight is all yours."

She followed Mary Jo to the dining room where close to a dozen women were gathered, either in chairs or standing around the table.

Mary Jo rested a hand on her back. "This is my dear friend, Eden Lambert, from Tallahassee. She's the genius and creator behind all the goodies you see here."

Several women hurried forward to introduce themselves and compliment her on the food. Names and faces jumbled in her mind as each new one approached, but Eden was left with the impression of kindly old ladies with tightly curled hair and wearing their Sunday best who offered her a warm welcome and sincere praise. She waited until she'd met everyone who came forward, then took a quick survey of the refreshments before ducking back into the kitchen.

Joe slouched at the table, arms folded across his chest and long legs stretched out in front. "So, how'd it go?"

She exhaled in a whoosh. "Great, as long as you don't ask me to repeat their names. They seemed really sweet. Not a wolf among them." She continued past him to the refrigerator. "And they must be hungry because we're already low on the chocolate and strawberry tarts. I'm going to take out some more."

He straightened, his soles hitting the floor with a slap. "Hey, I thought we were going to encourage them to eat the vegetables."

Eden laughed. "This crowd is more interested in sweets. They've eaten some of the fruit, but I couldn't tell that the veggies have been touched."

"Aw, man." He hovered at her shoulder as she assembled tarts on a platter. "Don't take them all. Remember you promised me one."

The dining room was pretty well cleared out when she returned. The noise had died down, indicating the ladies had taken the party to the garden. She set out the replacements, picked up a few abandoned plates and cups, and carried them into the kitchen.

While she was gone, Joe had filled a tub of ice and two glass pitchers, one with water, the other with tea. "Give me a hand with this, will you? If you can carry a pitcher, we can get everything in one trip. Once I'm sure they have plenty to drink out there, I'm gone."

He was obviously in a hurry to escape. She picked up the monitor. Jake was still asleep, but she knew it wouldn't be much longer before she'd be leaving too. She took the pitcher of tea and followed him outside.

The tall glass beverage dispensers on the umbrella-covered table in the center of the patio were nearly empty. Joe poured the ice into the lidded silver bucket, then took the tops off the dispensers and filled the tea and water levels back to the top.

"The party is only going to run another forty-five minutes or so," he said. "This should be enough."

"What about the drinks down there?" Eden pointed to the second beverage station they'd set up under a white canopy in the very back of the yard.

He followed the line of her hand, frowning as though he'd forgotten about it. "I doubt anyone has been all the way down there yet, but I probably should check them before I go."

She fell into step beside him, swinging wide of the clusters of guests ambling across the lawn. They were passing behind the tall row of hedges bordering the roses when they heard someone speaking from the other side of the shrubs.

"Mary Jo has really outdone herself today. The girl she has visiting has real talent."

Eden had only seconds to bask in the compliment before a second voice spoke. "She has talent all right, and from what I hear, it's not limited to cooking."

Joe would have kept on going, except that Eden grabbed his arm and pulled him to a stop. She put a finger to her lips to silence him and leaned in toward the voices.

"What do you mean?" the first speaker asked.

"Marilyn Bray told me the girl has a child out of wedlock and doesn't know who the father is."

There was a sharp intake of breath. Two, counting Eden's.

"Where did Marilyn hear that?"

"Apparently, the girl told her. I ask you, what kind of hussy had been with so many men that she doesn't know who fathered her child, then goes on to brag about it?"

The first woman spoke up. "I wonder if Marilyn has her story straight. I can't imagine Mary Jo inviting someone like that to stay in her home."

"Oh, can't you? What about that boy she took in? The drunk's son she and Matthew practically raised."

Eden had heard enough. She tugged on Joe's arm, signaling they should go, but all six feet three inches of him was firmly planted. He didn't budge.

"Joe Wolfe? He seems like a nice young man to me. So polite."

"He's a womanizer. I hear he goes out with a different woman every weekend."

"He's very handsome. It's not his fault there's no shortage of young ladies eager for his attention."

"Clara, you are so naïve. What sort of attentions do you suppose they are? A man like that isn't satisfied until he has a notch on his bedpost."

Eden turned slightly to see his reaction. His brows shot high, and a muscle twitched in his jaw. She feared he was about to charge around the shrubs and confront the old biddies.

"I hear he's rich." A third voice joined the conversation. "I remember when he bought the old Tyler place a couple of years ago. Someone told me he paid cash."

"And just where did all that money come from? He doesn't work from what I can tell."

"He has his own company." Eden recognized the peacemaking voice as Clara's. "He's a general contractor."

"So he says. For all we know, he's involved in something illegal. Say what you want, I think he's trouble. And the girl is too."

"Now, Eunice, I don't think you're being fair."

"I only speak what I know. Marilyn told me the police met the girl right outside the grocery store the day she came in shopping. Marilyn said they followed her out of the parking lot. If that doesn't sound like trouble, I don't know what does."

"Shh. Here comes Mary Jo."

"If you truly think her visitor is trouble," Clara said, "we should warn Mary Jo."

"She wouldn't listen. You know her. She only sees the best in people. I'll give her nephew a call. He knows I'm a close friend of Mary Jo's and has asked me to keep an eye on her. He'll want to hear about this."

Following a beat of silence, Eunice spoke again. "Oh, Mary Jo, we were just talking about your lovely party." Her previously harsh tone was marshmallow soft and dripping with saccharine.

Eden and Joe stepped back from the hedge. Rather than inconspicuously retracing their steps along the perimeter of the yard, Joe headed for a break in the shrubbery leading to the middle of the yard. Head high and dark eyes flashing, it appeared he intended to set the gossips straight.

Eden caught his arm, shook her head, and tugged him back to the edge. This wasn't the time for confrontation. Under no circumstances would she mess up Mary Jo's party.

They marched across the yard, their long strides matching over the stone terrace and into the house, going directly to the kitchen.

Eden swung the door closed behind them, hands shaking with angry, heart-pumping energy. "It's not true what that woman said about me."

Hurt from the unprovoked attack brought tears to her eyes. "I haven't been with lots of men. I was only with Jake's father. I loved him. I thought he loved me. I thought we were going to get married." She swiped at the moisture with the back of her hand. "What would make her say those things about me? She made me sound like a . . ." She couldn't make herself say the word.

"I don't know why she said it." His expression gentled, the anger she'd seen on his face replaced with compassion. He pulled out a chair at the table and nudged her toward it. "Just nasty gossip by a nasty woman."

"Don't you mean wolf?"

The slightest hint of a grin kicked up the corner of his mouth.

Thankfully, he wasn't the kind of man who said I told you so. She sniffled. "She said Marilyn told her all that stuff. Isn't Marilyn the checker at the grocery store?"

"Yeah." He slid into the chair next to hers and propped his forearms on the table, turning the full power of his gaze on her.

"Why would she say those things? I only met her the one time when I was buying supplies for the party, and we hardly spoke. I was fully occupied trying to keep Jake happy."

He shrugged. "Marilyn has a reputation for being a gossip. Around here they call her Mouthpiece Marilyn."

Eden pursed her lips. "She did ask me a bunch of prying questions. I remember thinking I should tell her to mind her own business."

He laughed. "Attagirl. Should have gone with your gut."

His laughter coaxed a reluctant smile to her face. "I *should* have asked her out for coffee and forced her to listen to the story of my life. That way she could broadcast an accurate report, instead of a bunch of half-truths."

"Seems to me she strayed into full-on fiction when she brought in the part about the police."

Eden shook her head. "No, she got that right. Sam was there but not for surveillance."

Joe's eyes widened. "Sam didn't mention it."

"Not much to tell. He pulled up as Jake and I were leaving the store and offered to help with the groceries. He *did* follow me back to Mary Jo's to carry everything in, but how did Marilyn know any of that? Standing at the register, her back is to the door. She couldn't have seen Sam unless she stepped away from the register to watch me leave." Eden grimaced. "How creepy would that be?"

"Anything for a story."

"And what a story it was! Complete character assassination. If words could kill, I'd be laid out on the ground. If that wasn't enough, then she turned on you. How do you stand it?"

He shrugged again, his face wiped clean of all emotion, the way people did when they didn't want others to see their pain. "Years of practice ignoring them. Sticks and stones—"

"Well, I'm sorry. I don't suppose it helps to know I'm angry for you." She stood and marched to the refrigerator. "There's only one thing to do."

"You're going to spit on the food?"

She laughed as she pulled out a tray. "Even better. We're going to eat it."

He made a point of looking at the clock. "I hesitate to mention it, but the party's not officially over for another fifteen minutes."

She placed the leftovers between them on the table and sat. "It is for me. Mean people don't deserve my cooking."

"Now you're talking." He selected a strawberry tart and took an enthusiastic bite. "These are amazing."

"Yes, they are." She lifted one in mock salute. "Take that, Eunice Welts."

CHAPTER SIX

Eden was really going to miss this place.

She lay in bed, savoring the tranquility of the morning before Jake awakened and the race was on. The first warm rays of sunlight filtered through the window, and she could hear the gentle chatter of birds.

She loved it here.

She loved this big bed with its decadent mound of sink-in pillows and the high-dollar sheets that felt like cool silk against her skin. She loved the sheltering canopy of frothy white lace that made her feel like a princess. She loved the old house with its soaring ceilings and creaking floors.

But mostly, she loved Mary Jo.

She thanked God, or fate, or the sheer coincidence that brought her here a week ago. When she'd stopped in front of the house to rest, she'd had no idea she would be swept into the orbit of an octogenarian dynamo that would forever change her.

Mary Jo had opened her heart and home to her and Jake without reservation. She listened without judgment and spoke without condemnation. She'd showered them with a love and acceptance Eden had never known.

She thought they were treasures.

Eden sighed. She was *really* going to miss Mary Jo.

Her original plan, loosely formulated, was to stay with Mary Jo through the weekend, then move into her own place in town. She'd thought by now she'd have scoped out the area for employment and housing. The baking for the party had taken more time than she'd anticipated, her own fault for creating such an expansive menu, and she hadn't had the opportunity to nail down arrangements for the future.

Even so, she was glad she did it. She'd wanted to give Mary Jo the very best, to repay her in some small way for her incredible kindness and generosity to a couple of wandering strangers.

The food had been a huge hit. Garden club members continued calling late into the evening to say what a wonderful party it had been and how much they enjoyed it. Mary Jo was proud and delighted.

Mission accomplished.

She needed to go before the nasty rumors about her houseguest reached Mary Jo's ears and erased the honor and pleasure.

"Mama. Mama." She heard Jake's chatter on the monitor.

She leaned back against the pillows, getting in one more good stretch on the silken sheets before she started her day.

She was really going to miss this place.

"Good morning, Mary Jo."

"Good morning." Mary Jo paused in the kitchen doorway to glance at the clock. "I really overslept. I hope you didn't wait breakfast on me."

Eden laughed. "Jake waits for no one. He's already gobbled up his eggs and a couple of muffins too." She hopped up from the table. "I kept your plate in the oven so your eggs wouldn't get cold.

Why don't you sit down, and I'll get it for you. Do you want coffee this morning?"

"Yes, but you don't need to serve me."

"It's my pleasure."

"May Jo!" Delight lit Jake's face, and he threw his arms wide. "May Jo!"

Mary Jo gave him a hug and a kiss before settling into the chair beside him. "I swear this boy is better than sunshine for brightening the day." She smiled up at Eden when she placed her plate and coffee on the table in front of her. "What a blessing to have you both here with me."

Eden pulled out the chair across from her. "It's been wonderful."

Mary Jo looked thoughtful as she scooped up a bit of eggs. "I guess with everything that's happened, we need to reevaluate our plans."

Eden froze halfway to her seat. *Oh no. The rumors must have already reached her.* She straightened. "Jake and I can be packed and gone in less than an hour."

Mary Jo put down her fork to give her a puzzled look. "Why would you do that? I was about to suggest you stay a bit longer because you haven't had a chance to look around town yet."

So she hadn't heard. Eden would have to share the shameful story. She lowered into the chair and dropped her gaze to her hands. "I overheard some women talking at the party yesterday. They were repeating things the checker from the grocery store had said about me. Ugly things."

"Marilyn said ugly things about you?"

Eden nodded and lifted her eyes to meet Mary Jo's. "But I want you to know, they aren't true."

Mary Jo sighed and reached over to take her hand. "I'm so sorry. I'll tell you, that girl missed her calling. She should have been a tabloid reporter. One part truth to ten parts filth. What I don't understand is why anyone would choose to repeat it. I hate to be unkind, but Marilyn is not known as a reliable witness."

"The woman repeating the rumors was your buddy, Eunice Welts. From where I stood, it sounded like she enjoyed making me sound bad. And it wasn't just me. She said horrible things about Joe."

Mary Jo picked up her coffee cup and took a sip. "Eunice is an unhappy woman. In her defense, she's had some disappointments in her life. Unfortunately, she's become very bitter, especially toward me. She pretends to be my friend to my face, but behind my back, well, I'm just glad she doesn't carry a knife."

Eden laughed.

"She also dislikes the people I love. Yesterday wouldn't be the first time she'd launched an attack on Joe, but I hadn't expected her to go after you so soon." She turned distressed eyes to Eden. "I'm truly sorry."

"It's not your fault she's nutso."

Mary Jo sighed. "I wonder. You heard me say I wanted to take over as reigning hostess. I was teasing, of course, but a part of me really wanted to upstage her. And that's pride. The Bible is very clear that pride comes before a fall. I'm just so sorry my foolish pride has hurt you."

It *had* hurt, but Eden had been more concerned about the effect on her friend. "I just don't want my bad reputation to reflect negatively on you. You've done so much for Jake and me. The last thing I want to do is to repay your kindness by embarrassing you in front of your friends."

Mary Jo threw her shoulders back and jutted out her chin in a perfect impression of warrior Aunt Bee. "I will never be embarrassed by you. You are a precious young woman and an absolute delight."

As much as she loved the affirmation, hearing the lavish praise made Eden feel like a fraud. Her life had been a series of screwups. She didn't deserve Mary Jo's high opinion. "I've made a lot of stupid decisions."

"We all have, dear one." She nodded into Eden's look of disbelief. "Some decisions have more visible consequences than others, but we are all flawed and broken. Every one of us. The miracle is that God loves us in spite of it. He knows we're a mess, and He still wants a relationship with us." Her eyes flew wide. "Oh mercy, tomorrow is Sunday already, and I haven't taken flowers to the church for the altar."

Eden bent to pick up the spoon Jake had tossed on the floor, wiped it on the hem of her shirt, and placed it back on his tray. "It's not too late, is it?"

"No, although I usually take them on Friday. We were so busy with the party, and I forgot all about them." Mary Jo looked toward the window and frowned. "I guess I could go out and cut some now, before it gets too warm, but to tell you the truth, I'm worn to a thread. I hate to admit it, but a party takes it out of me."

Eden thought about the bouquets they'd scattered around the house for the party. "What about the flowers in the dining room? They're still fresh and already arranged."

"That's an excellent idea." The older woman tapped a finger on her bottom lip as she strategized. "They weigh a ton in that bowl I put them in. I suppose I could transfer them—"

"No problem. I can lift it."

Mary Jo brightened. "Would you do that? Bless your heart. If you don't mind waiting until nap time to deliver them to the church, I'll stay here with Jake." She grinned. "I might even take a little nap myself."

Deliver them to the church? Oh no. She'd only meant she could carry them into the kitchen. She hadn't set foot in a church since the few visits she'd made as a child with her neighbor. She didn't think she wanted to start now. Eden swallowed hard. "I don't know..."

"Don't worry." Mary Jo brushed off her protest with an airy wave. "The church isn't hard to find. It's just up the street. I can draw you a map if you like. Thank you. You are a lifesaver."

Eden delayed putting Jake down for a nap until his eyelids were so heavy he practically fell asleep sitting up. Once he was tucked in, and the monitor transferred to Mary Jo, there was no good excuse to postpone her trip to church any longer.

She took a deep breath for courage, scooped up the enormous arrangement off the dining room table, staggered out to her car, and stuffed it onto the front seat. She drove the couple of blocks to the church, pulled into the gravel lot, and parked next to a pickup truck.

Eden scanned the old, white wooden building. The closest entrance was a plain single panel door. She hadn't thought to ask Mary Jo where to enter, or even to whom she was to hand off the flowers. She could call her but hated to wake her if she was napping. She'd just have to figure it out for herself. With luck, the truck beside her belonged to the custodian, and she could leave the arrangement with him at the door.

She hefted the bowl of blooms and started for the entrance. Two feet from her destination, the door swung wide and a young couple stepped outside.

"Oh, hey, let me help you with that." The guy, a hunky athletic type in a polo and khakis, took the arrangement from her.

The woman with him, a pretty brunette in a pink sundress, glanced at the flowers before turning a warm smile on Eden. "Those must be from Mary Jo. That means you must be Eden."

The small-town communication network was mind-boggling. Eden smiled. "Wow. You're good."

"I had help. Joe told us about you."

Uh-oh. Eden's smile slipped a notch. "You may as well admit it. He told you I was trouble, didn't he?"

The woman laughed. "He said, and I quote, 'She is the most beautiful woman I've ever seen.'"

Eden blinked. "Really? He said that?"

She nodded. "Yep. *Then* he said you're trouble."

The three of them shared a good laugh.

The guy shifted the flowers so he could extend a hand. "I'm Trey Gunther. This is my fiancée, Hallie Nichols."

Eden shook his hand, then hers. "I'm Eden Lambert."

Trey nodded. "It's great to finally meet you."

"And probably a relief to see I don't actually have horns."

Trey laughed. "Joe's really a solid guy. One of my best friends. It just sounds to me like you and he got off on the wrong foot."

She gave them an easy shrug. "It's okay. He's devoted to Mary Jo, which makes him almost human."

Trey grinned. "He says you're a baker."

"I believe his actual words were 'she's an amazing baker,'" Hallie corrected. "He may have even used the word artist."

Eden felt a warm flush of pleasure. "I don't know about amazing or artist, but I do love to bake. I was hoping you had a bakery here in town. My son and I are looking for a place to relocate and since I have work experience with a bakery, I planned to find a job in one."

Hallie frowned and shook her head. "The closest bakery is half an hour away in Corsicana. I know this because we are getting married in September, and we're trying to find someone to do our wedding cake."

"That's wonderful. Congratulations."

The door opened again, and an elderly man poked his head out. "I thought I heard talking. Don't tell me you're having a party and forgot to invite me."

"Come on out and let me introduce you to Mary Jo's friend." Trey reached out an arm to include the white-haired man in their circle. "Pastor Dale, I'd like you to meet Eden Lambert. Eden, this party crasher is Pastor Dale."

Pastor Dale stepped down onto the sidewalk, locking warm brown eyes on hers as he took her hand in a firm grip. "Welcome, young lady. It's nice to meet you. Mary Jo called to tell me you were on your way with the flowers."

Though the idea of standing next to a direct representative of God gave her hives, he did have a friendly open smile and nice crinkly eyes.

Eden returned his smile. "Thank you. I forgot to ask her where I was supposed to leave them."

"I'll be happy to take them."

Trey transferred the flowers to his outstretched arms.

"If you've got a minute, why don't you come in and help me find a place to put them? Mary Jo usually takes care of that part. I'm not too much for decorating." Pastor Dale wrinkled his nose much like Jake did when she told him to pick up his toys.

She glanced past him toward the door. "Well, uh—"

"If you two will excuse us," Trey said, "Hallie and I need to head out. We've got an appointment with a caterer."

Pastor Dale nodded. "Go on then. See you both tomorrow."

"Yes, sir. Great to meet you, Eden."

"Bye." She waved as she watched them go, wondering how she could pull off her own escape. The only thing worse than wandering around a church would be doing so with someone who could probably see straight through to her soul. She darted a glance toward her car. "You know, I think I'll be going too."

He held up the flowers. "You don't have to leave yet, do you? I need someone to help me figure out what to do with these flowers. Our organist is here arranging the choir's sheet music for tomorrow's service, but I'd hate to disturb her." He gave her a hopeful look. "It shouldn't take but a few minutes."

Eden bit back a sigh. Why did she have to be such a sucker for lonely old people? "Okay, but I can't stay too long because my son's napping, and I want to get back before he wakes up."

Pastor Dale balanced the flowers on one hip and held open the door for her to enter. "His name is Jake, right? Mary Jo has told me so much about him. According to her, he's the smartest, best behaved little boy ever born."

"He is pretty great," she said. "And he adores Mary Jo. Of course, she's easy to love."

"She's a special lady, isn't she?"

"I've never met anyone like her. She opened her home to Jake and me when we were complete strangers. She treats us like family." Eden thought about her own family. "Better, actually."

He smiled. "Sounds like Mary Jo. The sanctuary is this way," he said, leading the way through a large open room and down a narrow, paneled hallway to another door.

Eden decided to run a thought by him that had lingered on the fringes of her mind ever since Mary Jo first mentioned it. "She told me God brought us here to her. Do you think that's possible?"

"I wouldn't be a bit surprised." He opened the door and they stepped into the sanctuary.

She followed him up the worn red carpet on the center aisle, stopping with him in the middle of the room. "Why would He go to all the trouble? Jake and I are nothing special."

"You are to Him." The pastor pointed to the front wall. "You see that cross? You are so valuable to God that He was willing to send His Son to die on a cross so that you could be in a relationship with Him."

"Mary Jo told me the same thing. What I don't understand is why anyone had to die."

"Excellent question. It goes back to the fact that God is perfect. Holy. The Bible tells us because He is holy, He must judge sin."

He caught her grimace and smiled gently. "That's a good news/bad news thing. It's good because He won't let murderers and child abusers get away with their deeds. It comforts me to know justice will eventually be served. The bad news is that we are *all* sinners and deserve punishment. We haven't all murdered someone, but anything less than perfection is sin. And the penalty for sin is death."

Wow. That seemed harsh. God must take sin pretty seriously. What must he think of her messed up past?

"God sent Jesus, His Son, to take the punishment we have earned. He died for us. Anyone who accepts His sacrifice gets their sins wiped out and has the privilege to be called a child of God." He looked her straight in the eye. "You are special enough to Him that He was willing to sacrifice His Son to have a relationship with you."

"It's hard to believe." That sounded wrong, so she lifted her palms to clarify. "I'm not saying I don't think it's true, it's just a lot to take in. Until I met you and Mary Jo, I hadn't heard any of this. Wouldn't you think if people knew something this amazing that they'd be telling everyone?"

He gave her a grin. "Now you're starting to sound like me."

Eden's gaze traveled from the rough-hewn wooden cross, to the altar in front of it, to the colorful stained-glass windows running the length of the room. A comforting quiet blanketed the space. Beneath the lemony tang of furniture polish, the room carried the rich scent of history.

She sighed. "I didn't expect it to be so peaceful in a church."

"Really? What did you expect?"

She shrugged. "I don't know. Awkwardness maybe. You know, like that twitchy feeling you get when you go someplace where you don't fit in." She paused. "I haven't exactly been an angel. Having a baby without getting married doesn't seem like something a nice church girl would do. I don't want you to think that I slept around because I didn't. It was just Jake's father—" She clapped a hand over her mouth. Omigosh, what was she doing?

"You thought God would meet you at the door with a lightning bolt?"

She chuckled in spite of her embarrassment. "Yeah, something like that."

"I believe that if we could get a glimpse of God's face right now, we would see Him wearing an ear-to-ear grin and pointing you out to His angels saying, 'That's my beloved girl, Eden. Isn't she wonderful?'"

Emotion clogged her throat. She whispered past the lump, "You really think so?"

"I *know* it. Tell you what," he said, putting down the arrangement on a pew to pull a piece of paper and pen from his shirt pocket. "I'm going to give you a reading assignment. Mary Jo has Bibles at home. I want you to borrow one and look up this story." He wrote something on the paper and extended it to her. "After you've read it, I want you to come tell me what you think."

She took the paper from him and read Luke 15:11–24. "What's it about?"

His eyes danced beneath bushy white brows. "You'll have to read it to find out."

"Okay, deal." She tucked the paper in her pocket. "About the flowers, why don't we put them on the center of the altar behind the Bible. It'll look pretty and symmetrical with those big candlesticks on either side."

"Sounds good." He carried the arrangement to the altar, placing it as she suggested. He took a step back and looked over his shoulder at her. "Like so?"

"Looks great." She glanced at the time on her phone. "I need to get going. Jake will be up soon."

He nodded. "I've really enjoyed talking with you today. I hope if you have any more questions, you'll come to me or Mary Jo."

She was surprised to realize she'd enjoyed it too. "I will."

"Will you and Jake be at church tomorrow? I'd love to meet him."

"Yes, I told Mary Jo we'd go with her."

"Excellent. See you then."

Joe punched Sam's number on his phone.

His friend picked up on the first ring with his normal greeting. "Hey, Joe. What's going on?"

"I need to ask you a favor."

"Let me guess. You want me to borrow your new truck, right? Maybe drive it for a month or two, work the kinks out."

Joe laughed. "I've seen the inside of your squad car. No way I want doughnut crumbs smashed into my leather seats." He grew serious. "Actually, I want you to take Eden to church tomorrow."

There was silence on the line for a moment. "I admit, I didn't see that coming. Actually, I wish I could, but I've got second shift and won't be off until three. Why does she need me to take her? Won't she be going with Mary Jo?"

"Yeah, but I think she's going to need backup. Marilyn's been blabbing some nasty stuff about her, and I'm afraid she'll be the number one topic at church."

"Aw man, what is Marilyn's problem?"

"I don't know, but it ticks me off, especially when she made the poor kid her target."

More silence. "Poor kid? Did I hear you right? Are we talking about the same would-be thief with possible homicidal tendencies? Don't tell me you're going soft on Eden."

"Not at all. I just hate to see anyone get picked on."

Sam sighed. "Yeah, me too. I'm sorry. I wish I could take her, but duty calls. Since I agree with you that she'll need a shield, I think you're going to have to step up to the plate this time."

"That's what I was afraid of."

"And remember, if you need someone to put some miles on that sweet ride, I'm your man."

"In your dreams." Joe laughed and disconnected the call.

Well, darn.

CHAPTER SEVEN

Joe's alarm went off at seven and for a bleary moment, he couldn't remember why he'd set it. It was Sunday, a day to kick back and take it easy, to spend a couple of hours drinking fancy coffee and catching up with national sports on the internet. The reason for the alarm came to him in an unpleasant rush—he was taking the ladies to church.

He scrubbed his hands over his face and sat up with a groan. Of all the ways he liked to spend his Sundays, going to church wasn't in his top ten. Actually, it didn't make the list.

He used to go to church when Matthew was alive. He and Mary Jo would pick Joe up on Sunday morning and make a day of it. Sunday school, worship service, and then out to lunch at someplace fancy in Corsicana.

He'd sit on the pew between them, wearing the nice clothes they'd bought him and pretending they were his mom and dad. Since he sat in the middle, it was his job to look up the songs and hold the hymnal for them to share when they stood to sing. Matthew, God bless him, couldn't carry a tune, but what he'd lacked in talent, he'd made up in volume. He'd called it a joyful noise. The old memory still had the power to bring a smile to Joe's face.

After Matthew died, Joe and Mary Jo continued attending church together as they waded through the mire of loss and grief.

He'd held the hymnal for the two of them, and they sang the songs, though they agreed it never sounded quite right without Matthew's off-key contribution.

Eventually, Mary Jo found her way to the widows' group and the six or seven of them sat together during the service, making him superfluous. Though she'd assured him he was always welcome, he hadn't wanted to be in the way. She was entering a new phase of her life, and the fellowship with those women would be important.

Besides, he wasn't that crazy about singing now that Matthew was gone.

He showered and headed to the closet to find something to wear. Jeans were out. Even though most of the civilized world now attended worship in denim, he knew it would never pass muster with Mary Jo.

He pushed the hangers aside to get to the dress clothes in the back of the closet. Tan slacks would do. He snagged them, a green polo shirt, and a pair of loafers.

He pulled up in front of Mary Jo's house a little before nine. He paused, hand hovering over the ignition while seriously toying with the idea of turning around and heading home. He hadn't told them he was coming. He could be kicked back with his coffee and sports in less than five.

He shut off the engine. Who was he kidding? He couldn't enjoy a latte if he knew Mary Jo and Eden were under attack.

He took the red brick stairs two at a time and knocked once before unlocking the door and letting himself in. "Good morning," he called. "Anybody home?"

"Joe?" Mary Jo bustled toward him from the direction of the kitchen, concern etched on her face. "Is everything okay?"

"Sure." He leaned in to kiss her perfumed cheek. "I thought I'd join you for church today." The way her face lit up, like he'd given her a valuable gift by offering to spend a couple hours with her, made his heart twist uncomfortably.

"That's wonderful," she said. "We'd love to have you."

He really felt rotten when she teared up.

Eden poked her head out of the kitchen. "Croissants are ready."

He brightened immediately. "Croissants?"

Mary Jo nodded and nudged him down the hall. "Doesn't that sound delicious? Eden and I decided to skip Sunday school today since it would mean leaving Jake in a strange nursery an extra hour. That left us a little more time for breakfast, so Eden is trying out a new recipe. She made the dough last night."

"Smells great."

He followed her into the kitchen. "I'm willing to offer my services as a guinea pig."

Eden looked up from whatever she was doing at the counter. "Pull up a chair. I made a ton."

It didn't matter how many times he saw her, she never failed to take his breath away. Tall and slender and unconsciously graceful with her blonde hair caught up in some kind of messy do, she was wearing the same white dress she'd worn the other day to the party, under one of Mary Jo's aprons and of course, bare feet.

"Joe! Joe!" Jake sang out as he beat his spoon on his tray.

"Hey, little dude." He rounded the table to pat the top of his head, the only clean place he could see. "Looks like you're enjoying that yogurt."

Eden glanced over her shoulder. "My hope is that at least two of the four ounces end up in his stomach."

Joe surveyed the baby's smeared face. "Yeah, it's possible. I bet that's no more than half of it stuck to his cheeks."

Mary Jo moistened a clean towel at the sink. "Let Mary Jo get you cleaned up, little angel."

Joe pulled a mug from the cabinet and walked to the coffee maker. Eden edged toward him and whispered, "We weren't expecting you."

He ducked his head to keep their conversation private. "Last-minute decision. I figured I needed a dose of religion this morning."

She shot him a look of pure skepticism. "You're here because of the gossip, aren't you?"

Looks and brains too. He shrugged.

"Do you think there will be talk at church?" She seemed more resigned than worried.

He shrugged again. He wouldn't be out of bed on a Sunday morning otherwise.

She tipped up her chin. "You don't have to defend me, you know. I'm a big girl. I can handle it."

"Don't think of it as defense." He flashed an easy smile. "Consider it a show of solidarity."

She searched his face for a moment, then stunned him by raising onto her toes and pressing a quick kiss to his cheek. "You've got to stop being nice to me. I don't want to have to change my mind and actually like you."

"Don't worry." He grinned, resisting the temptation to touch his hand to the spot where her lips had been. "We won't let that happen."

A stupid smile remained plastered on his face as he carried his coffee to the table and took his customary seat next to Mary Jo. Eden brought the platter of golden croissants over and set it down in the center, along with a stack of small plates and napkins. Jake clapped.

"They look delicious, Eden," Mary Jo said. "Let's say a blessing so we can eat."

Eden picked up her coffee from the counter before moving to her place and sitting. She sent Joe a smile when she extended her hand to him and bowed her head.

"Lord, thank You for your many gifts, three of which are sitting around this table with me. Would You bless this food and the service today? It's in Jesus's precious name that I pray. Amen."

"Amen," Jake said.

Joe picked up a croissant off the stack. "Aww, man, they're still warm." He broke off a flaky corner and popped it into his mouth. His eyes drifted shut while he chewed. "These are amazing. No kidding, I think this might be a new high point for my taste buds."

Eden smiled. "Thank you. Don't you want butter on it?"

"Doesn't need it. They are perfect straight up." He took another bite. "I didn't know people made croissants."

Mary Jo giggled. "Where did you think they came from?"

He shrugged. "I dunno. Little French elves in a tree?"

They all laughed.

Eden placed several pieces on Jake's tray. "I'm thinking of making them with chocolate next time."

"Good plan," Joe said. "I will make myself available for tasting with ten minutes' notice."

The carefree, contented feeling that settled over him at the breakfast table lasted until they walked up to the door of the church and he held it open for the ladies and Jake to enter. The blast of cold air conditioning replaced the earlier warm glow with a wary sense of alert.

Sunday school had already dismissed, so the fellowship hall was crowded when they stepped inside the building. The smell of coffee and buzz of conversations filled the room.

"The nursery is over here." Mary Jo directed them to the left. "They'll be so excited to have Jake. We don't have many young ones anymore."

She led the way, with Eden and Jake directly behind her, and he followed several paces behind. If they were attracting undue attention, he couldn't tell. Mary Jo greeted several friends as they pressed through the crowd but didn't stop until they went down a short hall to a classroom with a Dutch door. A middle-aged woman in a bright blue smock stood behind the closed bottom half.

"Mary Jo, we missed you in Sunday school today."

"Good morning, Beverly. I have company in town, and we felt like an hour in a strange nursery was long enough for his first visit."

Beverly's gaze slid to Eden and Jake and her smile tightened. "I heard you had visitors."

"Here they are." Mary Jo wrapped an arm around Eden to urge her forward. "This is my dear friend, Eden, and her precious little boy, Jake. Jake will be staying with you while we go to the service."

"Okay." Beverly opened the half door to admit them. "How old is he?" Her tone wasn't hostile, but to Joe's ears, it was darn close.

"Eighteen months."

Beverly eyed the toddler with a distinct lack of enthusiasm. "Does he have food allergies? We usually have a snack of Goldfish crackers at about eleven thirty."

"Crackers will be fine." Eden carried Jake to the toy kitchen in the corner. "He has juice in a sippy cup in the diaper bag." As soon as he began to play with the miniature pots and pans, she whispered something in his ear, kissed him on the head, and exited through the half door.

"Don't worry, dear," Mary Jo said in a carrying voice as they retraced their steps down the hall. "Beverly is really very warm. Everyone says she is wonderful with children."

Joe followed the ladies when they made their way back into the main gathering area. The crowd had thinned out as people headed to the sanctuary, but several clusters lingered over their coffee and conversation. Joe, Mary Jo, and Eden were passing behind one of the groups when Joe heard a woman say, "I heard she's a tramp."

He saw Eden stiffen, and he closed the distance between them to place his hand on her back. She acknowledged him with a slight turn of her head and the ghost of a smile.

They were nearly clear of the group when a second woman said in a loud whisper, "You know, she's getting on in years. It's not uncommon to hear about people taking advantage of the elderly."

He bent and whispered in Eden's ear. "Ignore them."

The buzzing suddenly stopped. Apparently they had been discovered. The room was dead silent, except for the sound of their footfalls on the linoleum. Joe swore he could feel the weight of a dozen stares on the back of his head while they crossed to the far side of the room and the door leading into the sanctuary.

"Well, that was fun," Eden said under her breath when he opened the door and stepped aside for them to enter. "I wish I'd thought to wear a scarlet A on my chest."

He looked down at her and smiled. Her color was high, but she appeared more mad than hurt.

"What did you say, honey?" Mary Jo asked.

"Is it okay if we sit toward the back?" Eden said.

"I think that's a wonderful idea." Mary Jo was all smiles, nodding and waving to her friends, as she led them down the side aisle to the third pew from the back. She seemed completely unfazed by the stir they were causing. She was either oblivious, or a consummate actress. He'd never known her to be oblivious. "How's this?" she asked.

"Perfect."

Mary Jo slid in, Joe followed her, and Eden scooted in beside him. Mary Jo leaned toward them to say, "I'm so glad you two are here with me."

Eden smoothed her dress with a brush of her hand. "That makes one of you."

Joe tried to cover his snort of laughter with a cough.

The organist began the first hymn, and everyone stood. Joe flipped to the page and supported the hymnal so all three of them could see it.

Only Mary Jo sang.

Pastor Dale came forward after the song, stopping in the center aisle in front of the altar, and led them in prayer. He read the week's announcements, called out the birthdays and anniversaries the congregation was celebrating that week, and asked for prayer requests. When the last person finished speaking, Dale looked to the back of the sanctuary and smiled broadly.

"I'm so pleased to have two very special guests in our service this morning. I see Joe Wolfe back there." He paused, probably because he knew he couldn't be heard over the creaking and shuffling as the entire room turned around to stare. "I don't know if you all are aware of it, but Joe and I go back a long way. He is a true gentleman and friend, and to this day, he's one of the first people I call when I need something done around the church or the parsonage. Not only is Joe a skilled handyman, he refuses to take a dime for his work, which fits nicely into our budget."

The congregation laughed.

"Beside him, I see Mary Jo's guest and my new friend, Eden Lambert. I had the pleasure of talking with Eden yesterday, and I was very impressed by her keen interest in spiritual matters. It's great to have you both here."

More creaking and shuffling as everyone shifted their bodies and attention back to the front of the room. The organist started the next hymn. Joe found the page, and this time the three of them sang. Well, at least he and Mary Jo were singing. He wasn't sure what Eden was doing. She was either improvising because she was unfamiliar with the tune or just a really bad singer.

He shot a smile to Mary Jo. She winked and smiled back.

Eden put Jake in the high chair and sat at the table just as the waitress arrived.

"Welcome to Estelle's." The sixtyish woman with a pair of half-glasses perched on the end of her nose looked up from her pad of paper and glanced around at the group. "Oh hi, Mary Jo, Joe. I didn't see you come in." Her gaze traveled from them to Eden and Jake. "You've got company today. Somebody needs to introduce me to these beautiful people."

Mary Jo smiled and greeted her friend. "This is my friend Eden Lambert and her son Jake. They are visiting me from Tallahassee."

The waitress met Eden's eyes and gave her a warm, friendly smile. "Welcome. I'm pleased to meet you. Your boy there might be the prettiest little baby I've ever seen. Those blue eyes and blonde curls make him look like an angel."

"Thank you."

"What can I bring you folks this afternoon?"

Mary Jo said, "We are all going to have today's special, and little Jake here would like the chicken fingers and fruit."

Estelle wrote the order. "Got it. What's everyone drinking?"

"Teas for the adults. Jake brought his own drink."

"Okie dokie. I'll put this in, and we'll have your food out in a few minutes." She tucked her pencil behind her ear. "Great to meet you, Eden."

Joe watched her walk away before turning to the ladies. "Well, there you go. We've been to church, yet the only kindness we've seen today is from the waitress at a restaurant afterward."

"It wasn't the *only* kindness. Many of Mary Jo's friends made a point to greet us after church." Eden noticed several of them had closed protective ranks around her and Jake as they stood in the fellowship hall after the service. "Trey and Hallie were very nice. And Pastor Dale is my new hero."

Mary Jo's lip trembled. She'd kept her cool while they were in public, but once they'd loaded into the car and headed out of the church parking lot, she'd fluctuated between anger and tears. "I can't tell you how truly sorry I am. I've never been as embarrassed as I was today by the behavior of the people at church. I hope you know I would never have subjected you to that kind of treatment had I known."

Eden pulled Jake's cup from her purse and placed it on his tray. "There were some pretty tense moments, but as I felt myself getting really mad, I remembered what they'd been told about me. According to the rumors, I'm a loose woman who brags about my lifestyle. I'm so bad that I have a child and don't know who fathered him. Honestly, I wouldn't be too anxious to meet a person like that."

"But we're Christians. How can we lead people to Jesus if we refuse to show His grace and mercy?"

Joe's lips compressed into a hard line. "They're a bunch of hypocrites."

Eden smiled at her loyal protectors. "It may have been a bad reflection on the people, but God came out looking better than ever."

Joe pushed back in his chair and folded his arms across his chest. "How do you figure that?"

She glanced around to be certain she wouldn't be over-heard by the nearby tables before leaning in. "Mary Jo and Pastor Dale have been telling me that everyone is broken, but I couldn't see it. I'm the college dropout alone with a kid. No home. No job. Questionable future. Basically, the worst mess-up ever. So, I'm asking myself how could God love someone like me?" A grin split her face. "Then I saw the church people today, all mean and gossipy, and I realized these are my people. They need a Savior as much as I do. If He is forgiving enough to want a relationship with them, then there's no reason why He wouldn't want one with me too."

Joe snorted, but some of the tension had eased from his expression. "That's one heck of a revelation."

"While we're on the subject of revelations, it appears some of us are not nearly the bad boys we make ourselves out to be." She leveled a stare at him while drumming her fingers on the table. "What's this about being on the pastor's speed dial?"

Mr. Cool looked decidedly uncomfortable. "It's nothing. I don't know why he had to bring that up."

Eden laughed. "I think he sensed the mood of the crowd and was trying to sway public opinion in our favor so we could get out alive." She turned to Mary Jo. "Are you sorry you've taken up with such a disreputable group?"

The older woman smiled fondly. "Not at all."

"She can't seem to help it." Joe winked at Mary Jo. "She's drawn to people like us."

Eden's gaze encompassed them both. "I've never heard the story of how you two met."

"That's because Mary Jo doesn't like to tell it." He grinned. "It was not my finest hour."

In response to the question on Eden's face, he said, "I'd been caught shoplifting at the grocery store, and she intervened before the manager could call the cops."

She felt her jaw drop. "Shoplifting?"

"Yeah. I'd stuck a package of hamburger under my shirt, and the manager saw me. He had me by the arm and was dragging me to his office to call the police when Mary Jo appeared and demanded to know what he was doing. After patiently explaining to her he'd caught me stealing, she informed him he'd made a terrible mistake. She told him I wasn't stealing, but merely picking up the hamburger for her as she'd asked me to do." He chuckled. "There's no way the guy believed her. I mean, he saw me stuff it into my shirt, but she was so sweetly adamant, he had no choice but to let me go."

"How old were you?"

"Ten."

Eden frowned. "I can see a package of gum or a candy bar, but why would a ten-year-old steal meat?"

"I was hungry."

Oh. He hadn't done it on a dare or a mischievous whim. He'd done it to eat. Mary Jo had mentioned Joe's father had been an alcoholic, but until this moment, Eden hadn't thought about the day-to-day ramifications for a young boy. Tears for the injustice done to a child pooled in her eyes. She pulled a paper napkin out of the dispenser on the table and blotted them. "I take back every evil thing I've said or thought about you."

He laughed. "Don't feel sorry for me. That was the best day of my life. Mary Jo took me to Estelle's, bought me an enormous lunch, and promised I'd never go hungry again." He laid his hand over Mary Jo's and gave it a squeeze. "I gave up my life of crime and gained a family."

Fresh tears spilled over. "Mary Jo has a gift for that. Bringing people into the family."

Eden put Jake to bed at a little past seven, aware this would be the last time she would perform the bedtime ritual here. It had been a long, emotionally challenging sort of day, and she was exhausted. She needed to pack so they could make an early start after breakfast tomorrow. But first, she wanted to talk to Mary Jo.

She moved silently down the stairs and into the living room.

Mary Jo looked up from the magazine she was reading. "Did you get that sweet angel tucked in?"

"He went down without a peep. Thank you for reading his stories to him tonight."

Mary Jo grinned. "It was my pleasure. Especially since that's the only time he'll sit still long enough for me to hold him."

Eden frowned. She couldn't think of a way to soften her news, so she inhaled deeply and plunged ahead. "Jake and I are going to leave tomorrow, like we originally planned."

Mary Jo lowered the magazine, and her smile crumpled. "No, no." She shook her head. "Not yet. You haven't had an opportunity to look over Village Green and see if it would be a good place for you to live."

"I've seen enough to know that even though it's a great town with some really nice people, there's no work for me here. The closest bakery is half an hour away, and this morning after church, the owner of the day care was quick to tell me she wasn't hiring."

"Yes, but I bet we could find you a job if you were willing to drive a bit." Mary Jo sat forward, bobbing her head as though struck by fresh inspiration. "Sure, you could work in Corsicana and commute back and forth from here every day."

Eden could almost hear the whispers about how she was taking advantage of Mary Jo's hospitality. "No, I don't think so. I don't know where we'll end up, but I think it'll be best in the long run for us to live and work in the same town."

"But I have all this room here, and I love having you and Jake live with me." Her voice wavered. "I think we make great roommates."

Eden dropped to the sofa beside the woman who'd become her best friend. "I do too. And we love living here. I can honestly say this has been the best week of my life. But it's only a temporary solution. I need to get busy working on our future."

Brimming tears brightened the blue of Mary Jo's eyes. "I'm not going to tell you it doesn't break my heart, but I admire your determination to make a way for you and Jake." She took a deep breath. "Is there anything I can do for you before you go?"

"Actually, yes. I want you to pray with me to be saved."

"Oh, Eden." The tears spilled over her lined cheeks. "Really?"

She nodded. "I'm ready. I've read and reread the verses you showed me in the Bible. Pastor Dale and I talked about the parable of the prodigal son. I know I'm a sinner and deserve punishment. I also know God loves me and made a way for me to be saved and called His child, through the sacrifice of Jesus."

Mary Jo dabbed her eyes. "You're there. You don't need me to pray."

Eden shrugged. "Maybe not, but I'd like you to. You're the one who first introduced us. It seems right that you should be included to make it official."

"I'm honored." She took Eden's hands in hers. "Let's pray."

They bowed their heads as Mary Jo spoke the simple words that affirmed Eden's faith in her Savior and her commitment to turn from her old way of thinking and living toward a dependence on God.

When she finished, she gathered Eden into her arms for a hug. "Welcome to the family, precious sister in Christ."

CHAPTER EIGHT

The mood at the breakfast table was somber. Mary Jo awakened early to fix a big farewell pancake feast, but when they sat down to eat, neither she nor Eden had an appetite. Even Jake seemed to sense something was off. He ate the food placed in front of him, but without the happy squeals and tray banging that usually accompanied a favorite meal.

They heard a knock on the front door, then Joe's customary shout. "Anybody home?"

Eden brightened. They hadn't said their goodbyes yesterday, and it meant a lot to think he took time out of his day to see them off.

He whistled while he walked through the house to the kitchen and appeared in the doorway with a wide smile on his face. "Ah, great. I'm not too late to eat."

"Eden and Jake are leaving this morning," Mary Jo announced in a dampening tone.

"Yeah, she mentioned the possibility yesterday." He took a plate from the cabinet and a fork from the drawer and carried them to the table. "Mind if I join you?"

"Not at all. I made plenty."

He sat and took a second to survey the table. "Doesn't look like you've eaten a thing." He scooped two big pancakes off the platter and dropped them onto his plate. He poured a puddle of syrup over the top of them, forked off a bite, and stuffed it into his mouth. "These are delicious. You girls don't know what you're missing."

Did he have to sound so cheerful? Eden put down her fork. "I'm not hungry."

"That's too bad. You really ought to eat something. You'll need energy for your trip." He took another mouthful. "How long you figure you'll drive today? What's the plan?"

"I'm not sure." She didn't want to admit she didn't have one, that she'd been too heartsick to formulate one. "It depends on what we find."

"Which way are you heading? The Dallas-Fort Worth area is nice. Lots of work opportunities. Plenty of housing. Myself, I'm partial to West Texas. It's a long drive, but it's beautiful out there."

Mary Jo's voice was full of disapproval. "Really, Joe."

He shrugged. "What? She doesn't know the area. I'm sure she appreciates some guidance."

Eden scowled. "I'd probably appreciate it more if you didn't sound so delighted to be rid of us."

"It's not that. I just know how eager you are to get started on your new life."

Mary Jo frowned over the rim of her coffee cup. "That doesn't make it any less awful to have you practically pushing her out."

He lowered his fork to give Eden his full attention. "Is that what it sounded like? I'm sorry. Tell you what. Why don't you let me make it up to you? Let me take you and Jake to The Green. We didn't get a chance to do it yesterday since it was his naptime."

She turned up her nose. "It's not necessary. We need to get dressed and get on the road."

"It won't take long. It might even wear the kid out so he sleeps in the car."

She shook her head. "No—"

"I insist. I can see you've got your chin up like you do when I've offended you. I can't let you leave with hard feelings. And I promised Jake I'd take him to the park, didn't I, little man?"

Jake mimicked Joe's bobbing head.

"See?" Joe pointed. "He remembers. It's never too early to teach him that a man's word is his bond."

Eden laughed in spite of her annoyance. "You're ridiculous."

"Come on, Florida." He hit her with a powerfully persuasive smile. "You can spare an hour. Take your son upstairs and get him dressed, and I'll help Mary Jo with the dishes."

He must have seen her determination wavering because he added a sweeping motion. "Get a move on. The clock is ticking."

Why did she let him bully her? She muttered under her breath while heading up the stairs with Jake. They needed to pack up the car and go. They didn't need to be wasting time with Joe. Especially when he'd made it abundantly clear he was happy they were leaving.

Not happy. Giddy. He was whistling, for heaven's sake!

She'd foolishly thought they'd moved past the animosity stage. She knew *she* had. He'd lulled her into a false sense of favor with his kindness over the last couple of days. She'd actually come to like, even respect, him. She thought they were friends.

Again her judgment in men proved faulty.

Who cares? She was done with men anyway. She had her son. And Jesus. They were enough.

She carried Jake straight to the bathroom to wash off the syrup he'd smeared everywhere. His pajamas were particularly sticky. She'd have to get a plastic bag from Mary Jo to keep Jake's dirty laundry. Whether or not they found a place in the next day or two, she'd need to stop at a laundromat and run a load of clothes. She could get multiple wearings out of an outfit if need be, but he went through a minimum of three changes a day.

She dressed him in a blue-striped romper. The fabric was extra soft and the loose design wouldn't bind him on the long car ride. She kissed each of his feet before fitting his little socks and shoes on them and carried him to her room so she could change.

She pulled on the pair of jeans and T-shirt she'd set out for traveling. She folded her pajamas and tucked them into her suitcase. All packed. She may as well wait until they got back from the park to carry everything out and load it into the car. Joe was glad enough to be rid of them that he'd cheerfully carry the stuff out for her.

She slipped into her flip flops, picked up Jake, and headed downstairs.

Joe walked in the front door. "Good timing. I just moved Jake's car seat to the truck."

She didn't bother to look at him. "Thanks."

Mary Jo came out from the kitchen, drying her hands on a towel.

"I left everything upstairs," Eden said. "I'll carry it down when we get back."

"That's fine, dear."

Mary Jo sounded a lot more cheerful than she had fifteen minutes ago. Maybe she and Joe talked, and he'd convinced her she was better off without them. Eden's heart sank a little. Maybe she didn't need convincing. After all, her own mother had been delighted to see them leave.

She followed Joe out to his truck, a massive dual cab, and waited until he opened the door. She put Jake into his car seat and buckled him in. Joe waited by her side, opening the passenger door for her after Jake was secure.

Instead of thanks, she gave him the stink eye.

He caught the look and laughed. "What was that for? I'm just trying to be a gentleman to make up for my earlier insensitivity."

"Hmmpf." She shut the door in his face.

They made the short drive in silence.

He slanted into one of the parking places in front of the old two-story buildings, directly across from the park, and switched off the engine. "Here we are."

Eden looked at the weathered red brick structures and remembered her first hopeful glimpse of them a week ago. "I bet there's a lot of history in these old places. It's a shame they're all sitting empty."

"You're telling me." His mouth turned up in a rueful grin. "I own them."

"Really?" She glanced at them again before turning back to him. "Why?"

He shrugged. "It seemed like a good investment at the time." He released his seat belt and pushed open his door. "Want to see one?"

"What? Like go inside?"

"Sure. Why not? You've got a few minutes, and you're interested in old buildings. They're kind of cool."

She shook her head. "I don't think so—"

"Come on." He climbed out of the truck. "You're going to be cooped up in the car all day. A little tour will be a nice change of pace."

She didn't know why he couldn't show the tiniest bit of regret they were leaving. She worked to keep the snippy out of her voice. "Okay, but we need to make it short if we're going to have time to let Jake play at the park."

She collected Jake and waited on the sidewalk beside Joe while he chose a key from a massive ring he carried and unlocked the plywood-covered door.

"Let me find the switch." He entered the darkened room and flipped on the lights. He held the door for her. "Come in."

She stepped into a large rectangular room with high ceilings. The air in the room was cool and stale from being closed up. The scarred concrete floors were swept clean, and the smooth unpainted drywall appeared to have been replaced since the last tenant.

They stood side by side, just inside the entrance. "Do you know what used to be in here?" Eden's voice echoed in the open expanse.

"Some kind of ladies' dress shop. It's been gone for at least twenty years. When I bought the building, I gutted it, updated the wiring, and hung fresh drywall so that a potential renter could get a better idea of the possibilities."

She moved farther into the room, Jake on her hip. "It's a nice size. Big, but not overwhelming. Once you take the boards off the windows, I imagine it has plenty of natural light. I wonder what kind of business would do well here?"

Joe remained by the door, arms folded across his chest. "I don't know. I was thinking maybe a bakery."

"A bakery would be nice—" She whipped around to face him. "Did you say *bakery*?"

He gave her a slow nod. "Uh-huh."

Eden's gaze locked onto his. "Do you know someone who wants to open one?"

His dark eyes lit up. "No, but I have a friend with bakery experience. I thought she might be interested."

"Me? Am I the friend?" Her hammering heart drowned out her words. "You want *me* to open a bakery in your space?"

Humor tugged at his lips. "Why not? It might be fun."

Fun? The man was a master of understatement. "It'd be amazing." *And impossible.* She sighed. "I'm not in a position to start a business. My life savings are just enough to keep food on the table and a roof over our heads until Jake and I get established somewhere."

He shrugged. "I figured you'd need a financial backer."

"Who would be stupid enough to take a risk on someone like me?"

He stepped away from the door and spread his arms. "You're looking at him."

"Is this a joke?" Hope and skepticism warred within her while she studied his face. "Are you kidding me?"

"Not at all. I think a bakery could succeed in this town, and I think you're the person to make it happen."

Eden strode back to him to better read his expression. "Why?" She narrowed her eyes. "I thought you wanted me to go."

"That was before I realized what a great cook you are and decided to keep you and your tarts close at hand."

She huffed out a breath. "Joe, be serious. Why are you doing this?"

"Brace yourself."

She pulled Jake tighter in her arms and took a wary step back. "Why?"

"Because I'm probably going to say something nice."

She rolled her eyes. "Maybe I should sit down."

"Not *that* nice."

"Go ahead." She prompted him with a nod. "I'm listening."

"I'm doing this because we're trying to grow the town. Village Green used to be a prosperous little burg, but when the interstate went in and routed traffic away from us, the businesses dried up." He spun the key ring on his finger. "We're currently in the process of trying to attract new people and businesses to the area."

Not exactly the compliment she'd hoped for. "I had no idea you were so civic-minded."

"Are you kidding? I'm a card-carrying member of the chamber of commerce. I'm sworn to look out for potential new businesses, or anybody dumb enough to want to move here. Since we've ascertained you like the town and can tolerate the hypocritical, small-minded citizenry, I think you're a prime candidate for residence."

She frowned. "Was that supposed to be nice? I'm glad I didn't bother to sit."

He lifted his palm to stop her. "I wasn't finished. In addition to your skill and availability, you and Jake have become like family to Mary Jo. Granted, she loves everyone, but from what I've seen, there's some kind of special bond between you. You're the daughter and grandson she's never had. And it seems to me the two of you could use a little family."

She cocked her brow. "You're not doing this because you feel sorry for me, are you?"

He wrinkled his face in a dismissive grimace. "What's to be sorry about? You're young, smart, and healthy. If you don't take my offer, I'm sure something else will present itself. I just think staying here and running a bakery would be a win-win for everybody."

It sounded good. Crazy scary, but in a good way. Crazy, scary good. "You've told me there's no rental property around here. Jake and I cannot impose on Mary Jo indefinitely. Suppose I decide to open a bakery? Where would we live?"

He must have anticipated her question. "I'm glad you asked. Follow me."

She trailed behind him, through the door at the very back of the store to a stairwell. They climbed a flight of metal steps, and he unlocked the door at the top and pushed it open. He waved her and Jake in ahead of him. "The place needs a lot of work, but with two bedrooms and a bath and a half, it would be plenty of space for the two of you."

The door opened into a kitchen. The floor was ancient yellowed tile, the cabinets a peculiar shade of minty green, and the appliances Mayberry era, but it was a good-sized room with a lot of storage and a spot for a table and chairs. He cocked a thumb toward a pocket door tucked in the corner. "Behind there is the half bath."

She shifted Jake on her hip while they walked through the kitchen and around the corner into an L-shaped living area.

Joe pointed to the right. "I see you putting a sofa and a couple of chairs in this spot." He turned and indicated the left side of the room. "You could use that little nook as an office."

Possibilities flooded her mind. *She and Jake could have their own home.*

"Through that door is the full bath which is accessible from either the living area or the master bedroom."

She peeked in. It would be tough to date the pink porcelain sink and rusty claw-foot tub since they didn't show bathrooms in old TV shows, but she guessed Andy and Opie would feel right at home.

She followed him from the bathroom into a large bedroom with high ceilings trimmed with wide molding. Eden walked to one of the two tall windows, and she and Jake peered through the glass to Main Street and The Green. "Pretty view."

Jake patted the windowpane. "Pretty."

"The room is big, but the closet's a joke." He sent her a look of apology. "I guess people didn't have many clothes back when they built this place."

Eden thought about her one dress and figured the closet would serve very well.

After she'd seen everything, they moved back through the living area and on to the second bedroom, a slightly smaller version of the first.

"This would be Jake's room," Joe said.

"What do you think, little man?" Eden checked it out, peering into the closet and out the windows before joining Joe in the doorway. She and Jake had always shared a room. If she took this apartment, they would have the unimaginable luxury of their own space.

Joe looked down at her. "You're awfully quiet."

Eden glanced around. "I'm speechless."

His mouth formed a tight horizontal line. "Maybe this was a bad idea. I know it needs a lot of work. I cleaned it out when I did the downstairs, but I never thought about it as a living space. The previous tenant used it for storage." He glanced around before turning back to her. "You probably want something nicer for you and Jake."

She shook her head. "Oh no, it's not that. The apartment is beautiful."

He snorted. "I wouldn't go that far."

"But it is." She let her gaze drift around the space that had already captured her heart and imagination. "It's spacious, and the trims and moldings are gorgeous. It has so much character and history. The views are amazing, and the commute would be a dream."

"So what's the problem?"

She met his gaze squarely. "I can't afford anything this nice." She needed to be honest but refused to sound pathetic. "At least, not at first."

His smile was back, with added wattage. "That's the beauty of this particular property. It comes free with the lease of the store downstairs."

A store of her own *and* a free apartment? Hopes and dreams spun dizzily in her head. This was everything she'd dreamed of and more. Way more. She wanted to be swept away by the excitement of it all, but cold, hard reality intruded. "We haven't talked numbers yet, but even with you as backer, I don't see how any of this is possible. For starters, it would cost an arm and a leg to outfit the downstairs with ovens and equipment and all the other stuff it would take to open a bakery. Surely a backer isn't required to finance the entire operation, but I don't have a fortune to invest." She locked eyes with his. "And I won't accept your charity."

"It won't be as expensive as you think. The biggest building cost is always labor, and you and I are going to supply most of it. Your contribution will be in the form of sweat equity. I guarantee it won't feel like charity by the time you've sanded and painted and whatever else needs to be done to get a bakery up and running."

She wished she'd paid better attention to the business classes she'd taken in college. "Okay, say we're able to build it out at a reasonable cost. It will still take a while to establish the business. We're talking pure expense with no profit."

He shrugged. "Right now the building is sitting empty. It's already an expense. Even if the bakery operates in the red for years, there is still the potential to one day recoup our costs and make a profit."

She tamped down her growing excitement. What was she doing? She had the responsibility of a child. No matter how tempting, she needed security, not potential. Solid prospects, not wishes and dreams. She sucked in a breath. "No. Thank you for the offer, but I'm not interested."

He looked surprised. "Why not?"

"Too risky."

"If there's any risk involved here, I'll be the one taking most of it."

"I know. And that isn't fair to you."

He placed his hand on her shoulder and looked her in the eye. "I'm an investor. Risks are part of the job. I don't gamble unless I plan to win. And honestly, backing you is easy money."

Now *that* was the nicest thing he'd ever said to her. Pleasure poured into her. "Really? You have that much faith in me?"

"Florida, I believe if you put your mind to it, there's nothing you can't do." His gaze swept the room. "I want to build you and Jake a bakery. Are you in?"

Eden chewed her lip. Could she do this? Joe thought she could. It was a huge risk. She might mess up. Crash and burn. Or she might create something wonderful. A good life for her and her son. Truth was, she'd never know until she tried.

She swallowed hard and nodded. "Yes."

He grinned and gave her shoulder a quick squeeze before releasing her. "Excellent. I'll draw up a business plan this afternoon on how we want to structure the company. Once I've got the details nailed down, I'll run it by you. If you're still agreeable, we'll meet with my lawyer and make everything official. In the meantime, let's get this little guy to the park."

Joe watched Eden and Jake running across the park and sighed in pure relief.

Man, that was a tough sell.

He'd expected her to jump at the chance to have her own bakery. Wrong. She'd questioned him at every turn. Honestly, he liked her even better for putting up a fight. He liked that she wasn't a pushover, that she weighed the pros and cons before making a decision. He liked her practicality and the pride that made her determined to earn her own way.

He hadn't liked that she'd scared him half to death. That was no token resistance. She clearly wrestled with her decision, and it could have gone either way. When she turned him down at first, he'd actually felt a little sick.

He thought he was okay with them leaving. Her life, her choice. He figured he'd miss them for a day or two, then go on with his life.

He tried to pinpoint the exact moment it became imperative to him that they stay. He'd gone home yesterday after lunch, content with the knowledge she and Jake would move on. He'd kicked back in front of a golf tournament on TV and waited to drift off in a comfortable Sunday afternoon snooze.

Instead of the pleasant oblivion of sleep, a hundred terrible scenarios played through his mind. *Eden and Jake broken down by the side of the road, or cowering in a rundown motel, or living in their car, or . . .* The list was gut-wrenching and endless.

He didn't get his nap, but he did develop an apprehension of the hideous things that could befall a young woman and kid on their own. It didn't matter that she was strong and independent. He knew all too well life had a way of kicking you in the teeth. He wanted better for her.

But there was nothing to offer her in Village Green.

Except, there was. Possibilities popped up in his mind like dandelions in a spring lawn. He owned lots of property downtown, didn't he? So what if the town didn't have a bakery. They could open one of their own. So what if there were no rental properties in town. All of the upstairs apartments were vacant. She could live in one of them.

He'd hardly slept all night as he pondered the angles. This could absolutely work. How had he missed it? Where once he'd seen dead ends, the opportunities now seemed endless.

If she was willing.

He'd arrived at Mary Jo's this morning with an agenda. Before he showed Eden the store and apartment, he wanted to know she didn't have a better idea. If she'd outlined even a vague plan for the future, he'd have stepped back. He wouldn't stand in the way of her goals. He hated to condemn her to a life in Village Green.

But, if she seemed uncertain or if it looked like she was plunging ahead without direction, then he'd offer up his Plan B.

Their conversation over breakfast convinced him he should at least suggest his idea. While she and Jake were upstairs getting ready, he'd run it by Mary Jo. To say she was ecstatic would be an understatement. He hadn't exaggerated when he told Eden she was the daughter Mary Jo never had. In a week's time, they'd forged a solid bond that seemed to strengthen both women. They were good for each other.

Eden jogged over and plopped down beside him on the bench. Several feet away, Jake ran tight circles in the grass and squealed with delight. "This park is really beautiful."

"Yeah, it's okay."

She turned toward him. "Tell me something."

He faced her, admiring the way the sunlight glinted off her hair. "Sure."

"Why do you stay? It's obvious you hate it here—you have no use for the town or the people—so why do you stay?"

Nobody had ever asked him that before. He went with the obvious answer. "To keep an eye on Mary Jo."

She smiled as she shook her head. "That's sweet. But I'm not buying it. The interstate is close enough you could hop on it from anywhere and be here in under an hour. You could live in a big city like Dallas with your choice of restaurants, housing, and a limitless supply of women."

He cocked his brows. "Trying to get rid of me?"

"Nope." Her blue eyes searched his face. "Just trying to understand you."

"Okay, then how about this? I stay to annoy them."

Her laugh cut short when she seemed to realize he was serious. "Who?"

He looked away, focusing on the expanse of freshly mowed grass. "The people who said I'd never amount to anything. The ones who knew my old man and predicted I'd end up like him."

"So you stay to prove them wrong."

He thought about it. "Yeah, that's right."

"So you own your own company and half the town, date a different woman every week, and have the devotion of some truly excellent people." A bright smile split her face as she lifted her hand for a high five. "Congratulations, Joe, I think you've made your point."

Mary Jo pulled her Cadillac into the closest available parking spot and shut off the engine. She tugged down the visor to check her lipstick in the lighted mirror, hung her navy handbag in the crook of her arm, and walked into Grocery Giant. Monday morning was a busy time for the store and there were only a couple of carts available. She selected one, laid her bag on the child seat, and rolled to the nonfood aisle. She picked up the two things on her list and headed to Marilyn's register.

"Good morning, Mary Jo."

"Good morning, dear."

Marilyn looked into her cart. "I can usually tell what's going on in people's lives based on what's in their basket." She swiped a bar of soap over the scanner, then the box of Band-Aids. "That'll be $5.18. But your basket is a mystery."

Mary Jo counted out the exact amount from her wallet and placed it in Marilyn's outstretched hand. "Let me explain. The bandages are symbolic of the many wounds my dear friend Eden has suffered as a result of the rumors you spread about her. The bar of soap has a more practical application." She plucked both items from the bag and perched them on top of the cash register. "In the old days, we had our mouths washed out with soap for speaking filth or telling lies. My dear, you need to have your mouth washed out."

She nodded to Marilyn, gathered up her purse, and marched out of the store.

CHAPTER NINE

Eden bounded up the red brick stairs and let herself into the house. Mary Jo looked up from her reading and smiled.

"Is he still sleeping?"

The older woman nodded and passed the monitor to Eden. "He's just starting to stir."

"Whew." Eden dropped onto the sofa, scooping her hair off her neck for better access to the air conditioning. "I got tied up at the shop and was afraid he'd be awake before I got here."

Mary Jo shrugged. "It wouldn't matter. I'm happy to watch him anytime."

"I know, but he's a handful. And you're already doing so much for us." She grimaced. "I'm pretty sure you weren't expecting to house us for so long."

"It's not nearly long enough. I love having you two here. As excited as I am about you and Jake getting your own place, I'll miss you terribly when you move out."

Eden let the balm of her words flow over her. She and her son were not a burden to Mary Jo. They were a blessing. Even with the mess and noise and disruption they brought, her dear friend would miss them when they left.

"We won't be far away. And we'll come see you all the time. Plus, we want you to visit us at the bakery."

"I'll be your best customer." Mary Jo set aside her book. "Speaking of customers, I wanted to run something by you. I'm thinking of starting a women's Bible study in the fall. I don't foresee a huge group, probably no more than five or six women, and I wondered if you would let us meet at your shop? I've been toying with the idea of holding it somewhere other than the church or my house. I feel I could attract a wider range of women if we gathered in a neutral place."

"Of course you may." Eden clapped. "I'd love to have you."

The older woman grinned. "Thank you. I think it will benefit both of us. I'll have a place to meet with people who wouldn't be comfortable in a church, and you'll have regular customers for coffee and croissants every week."

"It's a great idea." Possibilities churned in Eden's mind. In the business model, she and Joe had planned to serve her baked goods and the occasional cup of coffee. If they had groups using the bakery as a meeting place, those people would want something to drink. Maybe they should look at offering a variety of beverages.

"I like it." Joe had stopped his saw when Eden and Jake came through the door of the future bakery. As he considered her suggestion about beverages, he pushed his work goggles up on his forehead, sawdust clinging to his face. "I don't think it would require a change in the layout. We allowed plenty of room for the coffeemaker behind the cash register. We have the space to add more machines if we wanted."

"I don't want to be a coffee shop. I still want the focus to be on the bakery. But I think that along with a really good plain coffee we should offer a specialty brew. It might be fun to do the same thing with iced tea. Maybe make the specialty drinks a seasonal offering. There's a lot of profit in beverages."

He flicked her forehead with a gloved finger. "I like the way you think, boss."

Boss. Sometimes she wanted to pinch herself to be sure she wasn't dreaming. Two weeks ago she had nothing. No job. No home. No plan. Today she had an apartment, or she would once the inspectors got here, and a business of her own.

Paradise Bakery. They'd needed a name for the business when they met the lawyer, so she and Mary Jo and Joe had brainstormed over dinner one evening. Everyone liked the idea of playing on Eden's name, so Paradise Bakery was born.

Joe trailed a knuckle over Jake's cheek. "Hey, little man. Did you get some rest?"

"Mary Jo said he was an angel and that he was asleep in five minutes."

"She would say he was an angel if he robbed a bank."

"Good point." Eden carried Jake to the playpen they'd set up in the corner, far from the action and potential danger. "You're going to hang out here while Mama works."

So far her contribution had been negligible. The first week, she'd spent her time with Joe designing the layout for the shop. That was fun. He'd asked her what she envisioned for her bakery, and he translated her dreams to a concrete plan. They'd walked the building countless times, talking about aesthetics as well as work-flow. They'd spent time online looking at the equipment they'd need, applying the measurements to their spaces, and tweaking their design until dreams and reality met in a solid, workable plan.

Joe was not just another pretty face. The man was crazy smart about business. When she questioned him about it, he told her Mary Jo's husband had taught him everything he knew. She had no doubt Matthew had been a good teacher, but it was obvious to Eden that Joe had a head for numbers.

According to him, they could be up and running in forty-five days. Two weeks into it, Eden thought he'd been a tad optimistic. Looking around the expanse of concrete and drywall, it was clear they were a long way from selling tarts.

Last week, an electrician came out and wired the shop to accommodate the commercial appliances. This week the plumber was running pipes for additional sinks and checking out the existing bathrooms. Joe was well into building the service counters and cabinets.

It was too early for painting or laying flooring, and she didn't have his skill with carpentry, so she had to content herself with sweeping up after him. In addition to cleaning responsibilities, she was the official gofer and made several trips to Estelle's for cold drinks every day. The upside was she and Estelle were becoming good friends.

Eden had been hesitant to disclose her plans to open a bakery. She didn't want Estelle to think she was encroaching on her food service territory. When she finally confessed, the older woman seemed genuinely pleased. According to her, competition meant more business for everyone.

On one of her many beverage runs, she ran into Hallie and Trey, the cute, soon-to-be-married couple from church. She discovered Hallie was a public relations consultant, with a background in advertising. Hallie had been excited to hear about the bakery and agreed to meet with Eden to talk about logos, signage, and branding.

Eden picked up a broom and swept up the sawdust and board ends from around Joe's work area. "What have you got for me to do today? I need to do something to earn my keep."

He glanced around the room. "I think I'm going to move you and Jake off-site this week."

Her face fell. "Are we in the way?"

"Are you kidding? I wouldn't be doing this without you, and my man Jake over there is our mascot. But the plumber is coming, and I don't know what kind of mess he's going to make. Plus, I need to do some cutting. I hate to run the saw with the little dude around. It makes a lot of racket, and I don't want to mess up his ears."

"But I want to work."

He smiled. "There's plenty for you to do, just not here. We need to order the furniture. And once you talk to Hallie, you'll need to pick out paint colors. Trust me. You'll be a hundred times better at those things than me."

"But—"

He lifted a finger for silence. "No buts. We've only got a month to go, and we still have lots to do. We'll accomplish more if we work separately. Divide and conquer. Just call me if you have any questions. And I'll be over at Mary Jo's for dinner tomorrow night. You can get me up to speed then."

"She wanted me to tell you she's doing the cooking since you're working so hard. She also told me to tell you not to get used to it."

"So Mary Jo's got attitude." He laughed. "Seems like you're rubbing off on her."

Eden scooped Jake from the playpen and walked back to Joe's side. "Do you need anything before I go? Do you want me to pick up a Dr Pepper for you from Estelle's?"

"I'm good. I've got stuff in the ice chest. You two get going."

He walked them to the door and unlocked it.

She stepped over the threshold into the sunlight and turned back to face him. "Are you sure?"

He grinned. "Positive."

"You'll call me if you need anything?"

"Absolutely." He waved before swinging the door closed. She heard the lock click.

She stared at the plywood-covered door for a moment before turning and slowly heading to the car. She didn't know what she had to be sad about. Joe was correct in saying they'd get more done apart. Unfortunately, she'd gotten used to spending a lot of time together over the last couple of weeks. She liked being with him. He was witty and smart, and he believed in her—something she was not accustomed to when it came to men. He made her want to be her best self when she was with him.

It didn't hurt that he was nice to look at. With a tool belt wrapped around his snug T-shirt and jeans—well, it just didn't get any better than that.

She clicked Jake into his car seat, careful to keep the hot buckle away from his skin. "Home? Home?"

"Yes, sweetie, we're going home." She planted a kiss on his nose before climbing behind the wheel and turning on the engine. A rush of air blasted from the AC vents. Her cell phone rang before she could pull out of the parking space. Ha! Joe didn't want her to leave after all. She pulled it out of her bag.

Not Joe. Her mother. Eden sighed.

She accepted the call, pressed the phone to her ear, and greeted her mother.

"Well, hey there, girl. How are you?"

She glanced at her son in the rearview mirror. "Jake and I are good."

"Where are you? I thought you were going to let me know when you landed somewhere."

She'd told her mother they'd text when they got settled, but her mom hadn't seemed that interested. Still, she should have contacted her. "Sorry. We're still in Texas."

"No kidding? That's great. Say, what are the men like in Texas? I'm only asking because I just threw Lance out, and I'm in the market for a new man. Maybe a cowboy this time."

"Which one is Lance?"

"Lance Minson. My boyfriend. Well, ex-boyfriend now. You remember him. You met him before you left."

She remembered that she and Jake had been evicted from the apartment because her mother's current boyfriend felt they were in the way. His name and face were lost in the sea of previous boyfriends. "What happened?"

Her mother huffed. "He's a freeloader. When he moved in, he said he was between jobs, and I was okay with that. I mean, job changes happen, right? But it's been over a month now, and if he's done one thing toward finding work, well, I haven't seen it. So, I sent him packing."

"I'm sorry."

"Me too. He treated me so good. Like a queen. He even held the door open for me." She sighed. "I really thought he was the one."

Eden rolled her eyes. "You always say that."

Her mother chuckled. "Yeah, I guess I do. So where are you staying?"

"It's kind of a long story. There's no rental property in the town, so Jake and I are staying with an older woman in her home."

"Girl, that sounds dangerous. You can never tell about people, you know. They look all nice and decent on the outside, then turn out to be creeps. Like Lance the Mooch."

Eden laughed. "I'll be sure to keep an eye on her."

"You do that. And lock your door at night. I didn't raise you to be dumb. Oh well, break's over. I've got to get back to work."

"Thanks for calling, Mom."

"Sure thing. It was nice talking to you. Kiss that baby for me."

Eden and Jake had just entered the house when Mary Jo met them in the hall. "Goodness, that was quick. You must have finished early today."

"May Jo!" Jake squealed and launched himself into her arms. He rested his head on her shoulder, patting her back with a chubby hand. "May Jo."

She beamed. "This little angel just melts my heart. Come into the kitchen, and we'll get something cool to drink. Is Joe on his way?"

Eden followed her down the hall. "No. He wasn't finished at the shop. The plumber was coming, and Joe was running the saw. And he didn't want Jake to be in the middle of all the mess and noise, so he sent us home."

The older woman turned to study her face. "What's the matter, honey? You sound like your feelings are hurt. I'm sure he was only being thoughtful."

"I know." She shrugged. "I don't feel like I'm doing enough. It's my bakery, and I want to help. To top it off, my mother called. Talking to her always makes me a little sad."

Mary Jo sat Jake in his high chair, then fixed him a sippy cup of juice. "Why is that? Is she unhappy with you because you moved so far away?"

"No. Actually, she told us to go." Eden took two glasses from the cabinet and filled them with ice and tea. She handed one to Mary Jo and joined her at the table. "She and Jake and I shared an apartment. When her latest boyfriend moved in, he felt Jake and I were in the way."

Mary Jo's voice rose an octave. "And she chose him over her own daughter and grandchild?"

Her indignation on Eden's behalf felt nice. "Yes, because she thought he was 'the one.'"

Mary Jo's brows drew together. "The one what?"

"The perfect man, her soul mate, her happily ever after. My mom never married—my father ditched her when she got pregnant—and she feels incomplete. She's the kind of woman who needs a man in her life to be whole. A Mr. Right. For as long as I can remember, we were on the hunt for 'him.'" She paused to sip her tea. "My mother has a world of common sense about most things, but she's got terrible judgment when it comes to men."

"I'm so sorry."

"You wouldn't believe the losers she brought home." Eden shook her head at the still-clear memories. "She gets so caught up in romantic delusions, she can't see past the fairy tale."

Mary Jo rested a hand over hers. "That had to be difficult for you."

She nodded. "The hardest part was feeling like I was in the way. Even as a little kid, I knew I was a handicap to her plans. If I hadn't been around, maybe things would be different."

"It's such a mistake to think someone else will fulfill us," Mary Jo said. "Even my precious Matthew, who was the very best husband, wasn't enough to complete me. That deep longing inside all of us can only be satisfied by a relationship with God. People are forever trying to find substitutes, and they're always disappointed."

"The crazy thing is I repeated my mother's mistakes. I consider myself a realist, but when I met Jake's dad, my brain went to mush. He seemed so steady, so right. I just knew I'd found my happily ever after. I created this fantasy family for the two of us . . ." Eden grimaced. "I'm more like my mother than I care to admit. I definitely inherited her bad judgment."

Mary Jo shook her head. "From what I've heard you say, you two are nothing alike. Your devotion to your son is clear. I can't see you setting him aside to please some boyfriend."

"No way." Family came first. Always.

"You're a wonderful mother. I've seen you tell and demonstrate to Jake a hundred different ways that he is a valuable part of your little family."

"I try." And in parenting, she was confident she and her mother were nothing alike. She got the nurturing gene. Her mother did not. But in judgment about men, they could be identical twins.

Like this afternoon when Joe hurt her feelings by sending her home, it didn't take a genius to see she was getting attached. Spending some part of every day with him had gone from being a novelty, to a pleasure, to a need.

Stupid. Stupid. Stupid.

Falling for Joe would be every bit as misguided as her mother with any of her so-called Mr. Rights—even worse, since Eden clearly recognized him from the start as a womanizing bad boy.

In his defense, he never claimed to be anything else. He took the ribbing from his friends about his harem in stride. He scheduled his dinner dates with Mary Jo to leave optimum time for his social life. Even now while getting the bakery up and running, he was gone by seven o'clock most evenings to "see to" prior commitments. It wasn't difficult to read between the lines.

Joe had always been honest. If she was dumb enough to fall for him, then it was on her.

"You are nothing like your mother, dear."

Unfortunately, Mary Jo's statement was not entirely true. She shared her mother's weakness in judgment. But, unlike her mother, Eden learned her lesson. She'd made a man her happily ever after once. She wouldn't make that mistake again.

✫   ✫   ✫

Joe turned up the radio a couple of notches, letting the blare of country music fill the empty space. He'd done the right thing. Jake did not need the piercing whine of the power saw ringing in his tender ears, and he wanted Eden out of the way when he talked to the plumber.

Still, it felt wrong without them. Kinda lonely.

He snorted at the maudlin thought. He'd always enjoyed being alone. It would just take a day or two to adjust to them being gone, that's all.

A knock sounded on the front door, and a grin stretched across his face. Eden was back. He couldn't wait to hear her excuse. She forgot something? She knew he'd want a Dr Pepper later, so she went ahead and picked one up for him?

He turned down the music and hurried to the door, unlocking and swinging it wide. "You're ba—" The big man on the sidewalk was definitely not Eden. "Oh, hey, Austin. Come in."

"That was a seriously goofy grin on your face," the plumber said with the familiarity of someone who'd known him since high school. "I take it you weren't expecting *me* when you opened the door."

"What? No, I mean, yeah—" He walked him to the corner with the playpen. "Go ahead and put your stuff down, and I'll show you what we have in mind."

Austin's gaze made a sweep of the room. "So, you're building a bakery for that girl staying with Mrs. Piermont."

"Looks like it."

"I heard she's a babe. Blonde hair, long tanned legs, the works."

Joe clenched his teeth and gave him a careless shrug as if he hadn't really noticed what she looked like. "She's pretty," he said.

"I've also heard she's not too particular. Something about not knowing the father of her kid." His face lit with a lascivious grin. "Girl like that might enjoy—"

Joe pinned him against the wall, his forearm pressed hard across Austin's windpipe. "You heard it wrong," Joe said with cold precision. "Eden is a decent kid. A real lady. And when you talk about her, I want to hear respect."

The plumber tried to nod. "Okay, man," he choked out. "I get it."

Joe dropped his arm and stepped back, shaken by the intensity of his response. "Sorry, Austin. I overreacted." He scrubbed his hands over his face and blew out a breath. "Marilyn over at the Grocery Giant started the rumor. She doesn't know Eden or her story, only met her once, briefly, but she made up that really nasty stuff and spread it all over town. I shouldn't have taken it out on you, but hearing the lies got to me. Here's a nice girl starting out in a new place, and Marilyn comes along and trashes her."

"I'm sorry." Austin rubbed his reddened throat. "I shouldn't have said anything. This isn't the first time Marilyn shot off her mouth about things she knows nothing about."

"It's okay. I'm sorry I jumped you. It was uncalled for." He tried for a smile. "I'll totally understand if you tell me to take my plumbing job and stuff it."

Austin laughed. "Not a chance. I always appreciate it when you throw business my way. And I was out of line. You say she's decent. That's good enough for me."

"Thanks." Time to get off the subject of Eden. He had a job to do, and she messed with his thinking. "I drew up a plan for the layout. Let me show you where we want the new sinks, and you can run with it. When you're ready, I'll take you upstairs and show you what I need done in the apartment. And do me a favor. When you meet Eden, I'd appreciate it if you didn't mention the work you're doing up there. I want it to be a surprise."

"No problem. My lips are sealed."

They conferred over the plans for several minutes. Joe knew from working with him in the past that Austin was up to the task. When he indicated he understood what they were looking for, Joe told him to get at it and returned to the service counter he was building.

He slipped on his safety goggles and gloves, then fired up the saw. He cleared his mind and focused on the board, using the blade to trace the careful lines he'd measured out on the wood. No room for error. Measure twice and cut once. He didn't want to lose a finger or waste an expensive piece of lumber.

In no time, he was absorbed in the work. He loved the artistry and science of carpentry. Matthew had been his teacher and had passed the love of the craft down to him.

The thought of Matthew brought a smile to his face. He'd been a truly great man. What a privilege it had been to walk beside him.

Joe liked to think he applied the principles he'd learned from the older man when he set Eden up in business. She brought potential, a good work ethic, and skill to the table and needed an outlet. He had the means to fill that need. His capital provided employment for her, filled a void in the community, and if the bakery succeeded, would earn a return on his investment. He believed Matthew would approve.

He was less certain how Matthew would view the fact that Joe would have built her a shiny new bakery even if he knew he'd never see a dime, that he cared nothing about profit or bringing new business to town and everything about keeping the baker nearby.

Actually, he was pretty sure Matthew would be all in if only because Joe was doing what Mary Jo and he had done for him. He had been young and unprotected when they stepped in to give him a safe and secure place to live and grow. He wanted that same security for Jake and Eden.

His motivation was strictly platonic. Sure, Eden was beautiful and insightful and great to be around. Sure, he'd gotten tripped up a few times by those big blue eyes. And yeah, okay, once or twice he may have forgotten to breathe when he focused on her perfect mouth.

But this was not about attraction or romance. This was about friendship, about survivors helping survivors find their way in an unfriendly world.

He shut off the saw to check his cell phone. Four o'clock. He had about an hour's work left before he headed upstairs. Jake and Mary Jo would be hanging out on the terrace blowing bubbles right about now. Eden was probably prepping dinner.

He should call her and ask her how everything went with the furniture order. No, that was lame. He was going to see her at Mary Jo's tomorrow night. He could ask her about the order then.

It'd be awfully quiet here in the morning without them. She had a meeting scheduled with Hallie at Mary Jo's at ten. They figured it would take an hour, two tops, to work through logos and signs and color choices. Which meant she'd be done by noon.

If he remembered correctly, Mary Jo had a Bible study tomorrow morning. She and the ladies usually went out for lunch in Corsicana afterward, so Eden and Jake would be left to fend for themselves. After a tough morning of corralling Jake while conducting a business meeting, she'd be ready for a break. He could take an hour off and meet them for lunch at Estelle's. After all, a man had to eat.

He dialed her cell.

"Joe?" She answered on the first ring. "Is everything okay?"

"Yeah, sure." He sat on the sawhorse. "I was going over tomorrow's schedule and thought I'd take you and Jake to lunch after your meeting. We can talk about the details while they're still fresh on your mind."

"Good idea." She sounded pleased. "I'll text you when Hallie and I are finished."

Funny how knowing he'd see her soon settled him. "Perfect. See you then."

CHAPTER TEN

Eden opened the door of Mary Jo's house for Hallie. "Come in. Thank you for meeting us here. It'll make things easier to have Jake near his toys."

"I'm happy to do it." The pretty brunette crouched down to his level. "Good morning, Jake."

He flashed a smile, then ducked behind his mother's legs.

"He's gorgeous." Hallie stood. "Really, he's such a beautiful little boy."

"Thank you. He's a keeper." Eden ruffled his hair. "I thought we'd work in the kitchen. We can spread out on the table, and Jake can play in the cabinets."

"Perfect."

Eden took her son's hand and led the way down the hall. She directed him to his favorite cabinet and opened the door. He immediately started pulling out the plastic bowls and lids.

"Do you want something to drink?" Eden turned to Hallie. "I've got coffee or peach tea."

"Tea sounds amazing." Hallie unlatched her briefcase and laid out the contents on the table. "After I talked with you the other day at Estelle's, I had my artist draw up a few sample logos for you to look at. We love the paradise theme you and Joe came up with—it's a great tie-in with your name and easy to illustrate. It'll be the perfect foundation to build your brand on."

Eden carried two tall glasses of iced tea to the table. Her gaze fell on the stack of pictures. "Oh, they're beautiful."

The designs ranged from a sophisticated silhouette in stark black and white to a lush full-color depiction of a tropical horizon. Each sheet was divided in half, the top half showing the artwork in a rectangular frame, the bottom in an oval. The name Paradise Bakery appeared somewhere on each drawing, in a variety of font styles.

She studied the designs for several minutes before picking one up. "I like them all, but this one stands out to me. It's simple and classy."

Hallie smiled. "It's my favorite too. The softer shades of blue and green are pretty without being too girly. Do you like the lettering style? I chose it for readability, but you can use any of the fonts on any of the designs."

Eden tilted her head. "I like it. It seems to match the picture."

"What would you think about doing it in gold foil, instead of black?"

She squinted in an attempt to visualize the substitution. "I think it would make the logo look really special. Exclusive." She tapped the bottom of the page. "And I prefer the oval shape over the rectangle. It would make such a cute sticker to put on the white bakery boxes and bags."

"I agree. And since you brought it up, let's talk about ways you can incorporate the logo with your product." The women settled at the table as Hallie spoke. "You'll want logoed stickers on everything that leaves the store certainly, maybe a mural on one wall, something painted on the window to catch the attention of foot traffic outside . . ."

Over the next hour, the conversation flowed from packaging to furnishing the shop in a way to reinforce the brand and encourage customers to linger. Hallie was enthusiastic and knowledgeable, and while it was overwhelming, Eden felt confident in the direction they were going.

Hallie closed her notebook. "So, do you have any questions?"

Eden took a deep breath and released it. "I think I'm good. I'm going to see Joe later this morning, and I'd like to run the things we've talked about by him. If he's on board with everything, then I'll be ready to move forward on the logo. We can get the stickers on order."

"That's perfect. I'll leave the design with you so you can show him." Hallie packed up the rest of her stuff. "We don't need to rush, but we definitely want to get moving if you're going to open in a month."

Eden clapped a hand over her heart. "Terrifying, isn't it?"

"Yes, but exciting too." She placed her briefcase on the floor then smiled at Eden. "I have a good feeling about the bakery. I think it's going to be a huge success."

"Thank you. Before you leave, we need to talk about your fees. I owe you for your time today, as well as the artwork. Would you like me to write you a check now, or do you want to bill me?"

"Honestly, if you're willing, I'd like to barter my services for a wedding cake."

"Really? I'd love to do it, but you've never seen anything I've done."

Hallie laughed. "It might be risky if I hadn't heard so many rave reviews. Ladies who attended Mary Jo's garden club are still talking about your food. Even Joe, who's tough to impress, sings your praises."

"Thank you. It would be a huge honor to make your wedding cake." And a great way to promote the bakery. "When is the wedding?"

"September first."

"How many guests?"

"About two hundred and fifty."

Wow. Eden swallowed hard. Big cake. Really soon. No pressure.

If she was going to be a professional, she may as well act the part. "Okay, I have an assignment for you. Get out your bride's magazines and find pictures of cakes you like. We can either copy a photograph or we can change it around, but pictures will give us a good, basic idea of what you're looking for. Are you planning on a groom's cake too?"

"Yes, I think we want to go with the traditional chocolate cake decorated with chocolate-covered strawberries."

Eden nodded. "Always a crowd pleaser. Let's plan on you getting back with me in a week with some pictures, and we'll design your cake from there."

"Thank you. I really appreciate it." Hallie got to her feet. "I'm so glad you're settling here and opening your bakery. And not just because you're doing our cake. It'll be great to have you and Jake in the community, and I can tell already that you and I are going to be good friends."

Eden had sensed it too. "I'd like that." She scooped Jake off the floor and led the way from the kitchen to the hall. "We could use some friends."

Hallie walked at her side. "I believe you've already made at least one."

She thought of her hostess and nodded. "Mary Jo is the best."

"Yes, but I was speaking of Joe."

Eden stopped to acknowledge the truth of her remark. "He's been incredibly generous to Jake and me."

"You two are good for him. Joe is a wonderful guy. Trey and I have known him all our lives. We've noticed a real change in him since he met you."

"Like what?" She never tired of hearing about him, ironic that she couldn't stand him at first.

"He seems happier. Less restless, more content. He's one of Trey's best friends, and yet Trey would be the first person to admit Joe's a mystery to him. He's always kept a part of himself shut away. But since you and Jake arrived, he's become more open. Warmer." She chuckled. "He whistles."

The idea that her being here meant something to him, that perhaps she'd helped Joe in some way, after all he'd done for her, brought a smile to her face.

"The first time I saw you at church together, I realized what a beautiful couple you make."

"Oh. No." Her smile faded as she shook her head. "We're not a couple. Just business associates. The only man in my future is this little guy right here."

Hallie looked as though she wanted to say something but pressed her lips together instead. She smiled at Jake. "He's a great guy too." She stepped toward the door. "I'll get going so you can talk with Joe. Give me a call when you know what you want to do, and in the meantime, I'll start collecting pictures of wedding cakes."

"Perfect. Thank you for everything, Hallie."

She and Jake stayed in the doorway, waving as Hallie disappeared down the front stairs. As soon as she got into her car and pulled away from the curb, Eden texted Joe that the meeting was over, and they were available when he was. Knowing he was working with the saw, she figured it could be a while before he checked his phone. She was surprised when he texted back immediately, telling her now was a great time to take a break, and he'd grab a table for them at Estelle's.

This was not a date, merely lunch with a business associate. She'd spoken the truth to Hallie when she said Jake was the only man in her life. She wasn't going to repeat her mother's mistakes, which did nothing to explain the lightness in her heart as she trotted up the stairs with a giggling Jake bouncing on her hip. "Fresh diaper for you, little man, and some lip gloss for your mom. And we're on our way."

In no time, they stood just inside the door of Estelle's, scanning the room for Joe.

"Hey girl," Estelle called from behind the cash register. "He's over there by the window." She pointed. Joe was looking at his phone and hadn't noticed them. "He's already got a high chair for Jake."

"Thanks." She pulled Jake close as they moved between the occupied tables.

Joe glanced up and saw them when they were still several booths away. When their eyes met, he flashed a heart-stopping smile, bright white against his tanned face, and stood to greet them.

"Hey, you two."

"Joe!" Jake threw his arms open wide as he squealed with delight. "Joe!"

"Hey, little dude." To Eden's amazement, the man who eyed all children with equal parts suspicion and dislike, scooped her son from her arms as if he'd been doing it all his life. "I missed you today."

Jake's arms circled his neck in a hug. He pressed his face against Joe's and sighed. "My Joe."

Eden's heart tumbled in her chest. She could make a firm stand against a bad boy. But how in the world could she protect herself against that?

Joe fitted Jake into the high chair, a surprisingly difficult maneuver. Channeling two chubby, wiggling legs into the tiny spaces took a level of skill he hadn't appreciated. When the kid was seated and strapped in, Joe took his seat across from Eden.

"Thank you for your help." Brows high and eyes wide, she looked as shocked as he felt.

"You're welcome." He had no idea why he grabbed Jake. He'd never held a child in his life. And honestly, why would he? In his experience, they were needy, noisy, and frequently sticky. Mildly repulsive.

Something weird came over him when he saw them approaching. It began with his usual reaction to Eden. He'd been messing around with his phone, killing time until they arrived so he hadn't seen them walk in. When he did notice them, he felt the familiar punch of adrenaline—the whole racing heart and sweaty palms thing. Same old, same old.

Then their eyes met, and everything else fell away. The twanging music, the chatter of customers, the activity of the busy diner all faded to black.

He only saw Eden.

His focus widened, expanding the frame to include the curly-haired toddler in her arms. He stood as they approached, propelled by ingrained manners, but more by a sense of wonder. He was looking at the two people who had come to mean more to him than anything.

Emotions   swamped   him—affection,   protectiveness, possessiveness.

He was in way over his head.

Next thing he knew, he was spouting sentimental drivel and hugging babies in public. What was that about?

He needed to take charge of the situation. Time to pull himself together.

He handed her a laminated menu. "Glad you could make it."

Her smile went through him like a bolt of lightning. "Glad you invited us."

Oh man, he could feel himself going under. He forced his gaze from her face and blurted, "I'm never going to marry." *Nice segue, Ace.*

Eden shot a puzzled look over the top of her menu. "Did you think I was asking you?"

"No, no." He shook his head and chuckled awkwardly. "I just thought you should know."

"Okay, consider me informed." She shrugged as if his announcement made no difference to her and went back to perusing her lunch options. "I'm not really surprised. I mean, why would a man who commands a harem want to settle for just one woman?"

"What?" He frowned when he realized what she'd said. "No. That's not why."

Estelle arrived at the table, half-glasses perched on the end of her nose, a pen and pad of paper in her hand. "What can I get you?"

Joe nodded for Eden to go first.

"Jake will have the chicken fingers, please, and I'll have a burger, medium well, fries, and tea to drink. Jake brought his own juice."

"Same thing for me, please."

"Got it." Estelle slipped the pen and paper into her apron. "I'll have it out to you in just a minute."

When Estelle headed back to the kitchen, he slid his menu behind the chrome napkin holder, took a deep breath, and plunged in. "I'm a bad risk."

Eden tucked her menu behind his. "Who says?"

He studied his hands as he recited the shameful facts. "Statistically speaking, someone who's been abandoned by their mother and raised by an abusive alcoholic father is a bad matrimonial risk. Too much baggage. The odds in favor of me making a successful marriage are low. Almost nil. The likelihood of me being a decent parent is even lower."

After a brief pause, Eden spoke. "Whether or not you ever get married is entirely up to you, but the idea of making such an important decision based on the statistics of other people's lives seems stupid to me."

He blinked. Really? She could casually dismiss the self-sacrificing life philosophy he'd crafted over years of serious thought and painful introspection as stupid? Disappointment flared. He shouldn't have mentioned it. The whole discussion was a bad idea. "Forget I said anything. You couldn't possibly understand how bad it was."

"No, you're right." Her voice softened and her expression filled with compassion. "I can't begin to imagine what your life was like, but I can see how good you are."

Joe ignored the spark of hope her words ignited. "You haven't lived here long enough to hear the truth about me. Give it six months, and you'll be convinced I'm the spitting image of my old man, well on the way to repeating his mistakes."

She shook her head. "That's ridiculous. He was evil."

"He's my blood. Do you know people always said he could build anything?"

"And now they say the same thing about you." She nodded as understanding dawned on her face. "And you're afraid those abilities aren't the only things you inherited."

He thought about slamming Austin into the wall the previous day and shrugged.

"Tell me about your dad."

He grimaced. "Why?"

"So I can draw my own conclusions. What did he look like?"

He almost hated to picture the man. "He was tall—"

"How tall?" she interrupted. "Be specific."

"Not quite six feet."

"And you're what, six three?"

"About that, yeah."

"So you didn't get your height from your father." She seemed to file the information away. "Go on. Tell me more."

"He was a big man, played football in high school. He was barrel-chested with muscular arms and big hands."

"Please don't tell me he was hairy." She screwed up her face in disgust. "It sounds like you're describing an ape."

Joe's smile at her comment quickly faded. "He was definitely an animal, angry and withdrawn when he was sober, mean and belligerent when he was drunk. And he was drunk a good part of every day. He had a horrible temper. I was terrified of setting him off."

"And if you did?"

"He'd backhand me. Knock me down if he was really mad." Joe remembered the day he finally figured out it was smarter to stay down until his father left.

Unshed tears made her eyes appear even bluer as she continued her steady line of questioning. "Did he hit your mother?"

"I guess so. She left when I was a little older than Jake, so I don't remember her, but piecing things together from stuff he said led me to believe he beat her up. More than once."

"So that's why she left."

He hated talking about this. The memories made him sick in the pit of his stomach. "I assume so."

Eden frowned. "I wonder why she didn't take you? I mean, I understand her leaving to escape the abuse, but to leave her child . . ."

Her relentless questions exposed wounds he'd been hiding for years. "She tried. He told me she tried to walk out with me, and he threatened to kill her. He was proud of it. Somewhere along the way, he'd convinced himself she was the cause of his problems. It was her fault he drank, her fault he couldn't hold a job."

"So he kept you to punish her. He knew depriving her of her beautiful little boy would be the worst punishment of all." Eden's voice cracked with emotion. "That her heart would break a thousand times a day."

He hadn't thought of it that way. All these years, he'd focused on the fact his mother abandoned him, never on the cost to her to do it.

Eden pulled a fresh napkin from the dispenser to swipe at leaking tears. "Where is he now?"

"He died the year I turned eighteen. He basically drank himself to death."

"Good. I probably shouldn't say it, but I'm glad. Where's your mother? What's her name?"

"Ramona." He shrugged. "I have no idea where she is."

He breathed a sigh of relief when Estelle approached the table, balancing three plates in her hands. End of discussion.

She placed the plates on the table with a flourish. "Enjoy."

Joe blew on one of his fries to cool it, then handed it into Jake's chubby fingers to tide him over until his mother finished cutting up his meat.

"Fry." Jake bobbed his head while chewing a mouthful of potato. "Fry."

"Do you drink?" Eden asked without looking up.

It took him a second to figure out the interrogation wasn't finished. "No alcohol, if that's what you're asking."

"Ever?"

"Not a drop. Never saw the point."

"Have you ever struck a woman or child?"

He reared back. "Of course not." The thought sickened him.

She lowered her knife and fork to give him her full scrutiny. "Been tempted?"

"No. Never. Not even a little."

She dropped the neatly cut chicken pieces onto Jake's tray. "That concludes our interview. Would you like to hear my conclusions?"

Yes and no. He desperately wanted affirmation, even absolution from this woman who'd come to mean everything to him. But if after looking at the evidence, she chose to come down on the side of the town . . . "Do I have a choice?"

She shook her head. "Not really."

"Fine." He kept his expression neutral in a show of indifference. "Fire away."

"Barring some impressive building skills, which I doubt very much are genetically transmitted, you are nothing like your biological father." She waited until he met her eyes to continue. "You certainly don't resemble him physically, thank God, since the man you described to me sounds like the missing link."

The tightness in his chest eased enough that he could chuckle.

"More importantly, you don't respond like him emotionally. He was a cruel, angry man who preyed on the weak." She reached across the table to briefly place her hand on his. "In spite of or maybe because of your past, you are a kind, strong man who protects those who can't protect themselves."

Every molecule in his body wanted to believe her. "That's very flattering, but you've never seen me angry."

Her brows shot up. "Oh no? How about the day I met you? You were breathing fire when you found out Jake and I were staying at Mary Jo's."

He smiled at the memory. "Yeah, I was pretty steamed."

"You thought I presented a threat to her, but you didn't resort to violence. Other than a few intimidating glares."

He grinned over his iced tea. "I don't recall you being frightened."

"I wasn't. It was clear to me you were being a jerk to protect Mary Jo."

"Hey!" He lowered his glass with a thump. "I was just getting used to the idea of being a hero, and you're busting me back to a jerk."

The warm look she leveled on him reassured him his lofty position was secure. "You *are* a hero. Even the good guys have to be fierce in the face of threats."

They ate in silence. Jake finally slowed from stuffing food into his mouth as fast as he could to playing with the remains on his tray. Joe assumed—*hoped*—that Eden had finally tired of discussing his past. He knew he had. He liked ending on a positive note, savoring his newfound status as hero.

She dabbed her mouth with a napkin. "You're nothing like your biological father, but you have a lot of your adoptive father's qualities."

He gave her a blank look. "I wasn't adopted."

"Maybe not on paper, but certainly in every way that counts. I believe when Mary Jo and her husband stepped into your life, they became your unofficial parents. According to Mary Jo, you were Matthew's shadow, a human sponge soaking up every word that dropped from his lips. She says you're just like him."

He smiled. "I'd like to think that was true. He was the best man I've ever known."

"And I believe you're following closely in his footsteps."

She'd given him a lot to consider. First, he was not the only victim in his childhood. Hearing Eden's perspective and observing her bond with Jake, he could see his mother paid a heavy price by walking away. On top of that, in his fear of becoming like his old man, he'd downplayed the enormous impact Mary Jo and Matthew had had in his life. Nature versus nurture.

He may have the bloodline of an abusive drunk, but his values, work ethic, and worldview were 100 percent a product of the Piermonts' godly influence. If his father carried any weight in his life, it was only to serve as a warning about what not to do.

"However, even though you are entirely eligible, I don't blame you for not wanting to get married." She ducked under the table, picking up the fries Jake flung to the floor and discarding them on her plate. "Honestly, I'm not interested in the institution either."

He had no idea why her statement should upset him. "Why not?"

She lifted her shoulders in a dismissive shrug. "I've got Jake. I owe it to him to focus on him. I know what it was like to be pushed to the side so my mom could pursue her Mr. Right. I don't want him to ever feel he's in the way."

"So, find a man who wants the whole package—you *and* Jake."

"In my experience, that man doesn't exist."

"I think you're underestimating my gender." He tried another tack. "What about romance?"

Her snort was accompanied by an eloquent eye roll. "No, thanks. I'm a little old for fairy tales."

He wagged his head. "Florida, you are a cynic."

"I'm a realist." She reached over to capture Jake's hand and stop him from pounding on the tray. "I think we're out of time. I'd better get him out of here before things get ugly."

Joe waited until she wiped Jake's hands and face, then picked him up out of the chair. He tossed a couple of bills on the check. "I'll carry him to the car for you."

"Bye, y'all," Estelle called as they passed the cash register on the way to the door. "Bye, Jake, see you soon."

"Bye-bye." He waved to her over Joe's shoulder.

Joe and Jake led the way to Eden's car.

"Thanks for inviting us to lunch." She unlocked it and opened the back door, releasing a rush of heat.

Belatedly, he remembered the reason he'd asked her to meet him. "I didn't even ask you about your meeting with Hallie."

"It went really well. I chose a design for our logo. And I took a bunch of notes on things you and I will have to decide."

Jake rubbed his eyes with his fists.

Eden kissed her son's cheek. "I better get this guy home for a nap. We can talk about the meeting when you come for dinner tonight."

"Sounds like a plan." He angled into the car and placed Jake in his seat. "See you later, little dude."

He gave Joe a sleepy smile. "Bye-bye."

Eden brushed past Joe to fasten the buckles over her son. Joe inhaled deeply, capturing her unique fragrance of spice and sunshine. His thigh touched her side, and he could have remained there indefinitely if it meant maintaining the slight physical connection. Of course, that would be pathetic, and Joe Wolfe didn't do pathetic. So, he stood back and waited until they pulled away.

He waved when they drove off, only mildly alarmed he was counting the minutes until he would see them again.

CHAPTER ELEVEN

Eden buckled Jake into his car seat in Joe's truck and climbed up onto the bench seat beside him. Joe half-lifted, half-tossed short Mary Jo onto the front seat, went around and climbed into the driver's side, then waited until everyone was clicked into their seat belts before he cranked up the engine.

Mary Jo turned around toward Eden and clapped her hands. "This is so exciting."

"I can't wait for you to see everything," Eden said. "Now that the furniture is there and the inspector has signed off, you can help me decide where to put the plants."

"I'm sure it's all perfect."

"It should be. You wouldn't know it to look at her, but this girl's a slave driver." Joe cocked a thumb over his shoulder to indicate Eden. "She had me set up the furniture one way on Monday, switch it all around on Tuesday, and move it back to its original placement on Wednesday."

Eden bit back a laugh. He was smiling about it now, but at the time, he hadn't thought it was too funny. She could still see the expression on his face when she told him it was all wrong. "I had to look at every option so I'd know we had the perfect arrangement. Besides, you're being compensated in cookies and cupcakes. Think of the moving as a means to prevent those carbs from turning to fat. We don't want to disappoint the harem."

Mary Jo patted her tummy. "I guess I need to start moving furniture. I swear I've gained five pounds since meeting you."

"It's probably muscle from lugging Jake around." Eden grinned. "He'll be so spoiled from being carried everywhere, he won't remember how to walk."

Mary Jo aimed an adoring smile at the toddler. "Mr. Jake and I are buds."

He bounced in his seat. "Buds. Buds."

Major understatement. They were inseparable from breakfast to bedtime. Just this week, Eden noticed Mary Jo interpreted some of his baby talk better than she could. As much as she was looking forward to having her own place, she dreaded separating the twosome.

Of course, the way things were going, that day may never come. The inspectors had been great about the bakery but impossible to pin down about signing off on the upstairs apartment. Joe worked closely with them and assured her the delay was a normal part of small-town life. He promised she'd have her apartment by the grand opening.

Her apartment. She'd only seen it the one time when Joe first offered it to her, before he'd discovered the stairs leading up to the second floor required extensive repairs, but she could hardly wait to move in and make it her own. It needed a major overhaul, but nothing could dampen her excitement. With time and paint and garage-sale furniture, she'd create a haven for herself and her son.

Sprinkled into the excitement was a dash of sadness. Once they moved out, Eden wouldn't have the easy access to Mary Jo's company over meals or the long conversations after she tucked Jake into bed for the night. They'd already made plans for weekly dinners and slumber parties on weekends, but it wouldn't be the same.

Change was hard. Stepping into the unknown was scary. Fear and doubt crouched in the shadows waiting to spring. To paralyze.

It quieted her to know the same God who went to the trouble to guide her to Village Green would continue to walk beside her down this new path. Her memory verse this week was a promise from Jesus. "I will never leave you nor forsake you."

Every time she repeated it, she felt a surge of fresh courage. *Bring it on. I've got Jesus in my corner.*

Joe angled the truck into the spot in front of the bakery and shut down the engine.

Mary Jo gasped. "Oh, Eden. The sign on the window is gorgeous."

Eden disengaged her seat belt to sit forward and admire the shop logo painted on the bakery window. They'd gone with the oval design, the one with the words *Paradise* and *Bakery* framing a simple silhouetted tropical scene. "What about the gold? Be honest, do you think it's too much?"

Mary Jo shook her head. "Not at all. I love it. It makes a very elegant impression."

Eden released a sigh. "Okay, good."

"Hey, wait a minute." Joe swung open his door, then turned to glare at her. "What 'okay good'? Your business associate here has told you a thousand times it looked great, and you've been giving me that I'm-not-so-sure look. Mary Jo sees it for a second and says she likes it, and suddenly it's great and your worries are over?"

Mary Jo reached over to pat his arm. "Don't try to understand, dear. It's a girl thing."

"Girl thing." Joe snorted as he climbed out of the truck. He unbuckled Jake from his car seat. "Come on, little dude. We guys have to stick together." He scooped him up before rounding the back to help the ladies.

He carried Jake while Eden unlocked the shop and disarmed the alarm. She flipped on the overhead lights and held the door for the others to enter.

"Welcome to Paradise Bakery."

Mary Jo stood quiet for a moment, turning a slow, full circle as her gaze traveled the room. Ridiculously nervous, Eden held her breath until finally the older woman stopped and met her eyes. "It's absolutely perfect. You two have created a little corner of heaven."

Eden shared a triumphant smile with Joe before asking her, "Okay, give me your honest impression. What did you think when you first walked in?"

Mary Jo paused. "I felt a sense of calm. It's very peaceful here. The colors you've chosen and the uncluttered arrangement of furniture makes it feel very fresh and serene."

Joe clapped Eden on the back. "Congratulations, boss. You did it."

Eden sighed with pure joy. From the beginning of the project, even before the bakery had a name, she'd had a clear vision for the space. In contrast to the prevailing Texas-cowboy-western theme she'd seen in town, she wanted a coastal vibe. Instead of denim blue and bandana red, she'd pictured the blue gray of the Atlantic, the clear blue of a summer sky, the creamy white of Florida sand, and the golden brown of sun-bleached wood. She and Joe had brought the vision to life with white shiplap walls, ocean blue fabric on the chairs, and driftwood-toned wood floors.

They'd divided the room into sections, each with a specific purpose. In the front left of the shop, she'd placed two groupings of upholstered club chairs with a small table tucked between them. She left an open lane through the center of the room for traffic flow and placed a long, oak plank table that would seat six or eight on the front right. Thinking of Mary Jo's future Bible studies, she chose comfortable chairs in an industrial-looking metal to set around it.

The back left of the shop was the service area. After much deliberation, she and Joe settled on a cafeteria-style setup. He constructed a waist-high rectangular counter, topped with gray granite and divided with a glass panel to separate the customers from the goodies.

The back right of the bakery was set with three more wood tables, square with four chairs each.

Eden pointed to the long table. "We'll put your Bible study over there."

"Thank you, dear." Mary Jo crossed to it, silent as she ran her hand over the smooth surface and tested out one of the chairs. She turned back to Eden with a smile. "It's perfect." She pointed to the light fixture suspended over the table. "And these old eyes thank you for providing extra light."

Eden nodded toward Joe who was following Jake as he wove a path through the furniture. "That was Joe's idea. He suggested we keep a couple copies of the local newspaper available in the center of the table to designate this as a reading area. And see all these outlets? He wired the table so people could plug in their devices if they prefer digital media."

Mary Jo beamed. "Isn't he the cleverest thing?"

He must have heard her remark because he scooped up Jake, and the twosome joined them at the table. "I tell Eden that all the time. Maybe she'll believe it if it comes from you."

Eden rolled her eyes. "Don't let him kid you. I've told him at least three times a day that he is a genius, and I don't know what I'd do without him."

She said it laughingly, but honestly, there weren't enough words to express her amazement and gratitude for everything he'd done. She'd worked hard, but he'd worked harder. She'd put in the time, but he'd put in hours beyond hers. He'd met her every step of the way, fleshing out her dream into a brick-and-mortar reality. To top it all off, he'd bankrolled the whole thing. "I'll never be able to thank him enough."

He grinned. "Are you kidding? Just keep those tarts and pastries coming."

The perfect first guest, Mary Jo marveled over every detail of the room. She was particularly impressed with the corral they'd built for Jake, a small fenced-in area attached to the service counter where he could play safely while his mother waited on customers.

"It looks like you two have thought of everything."

"I hope so." Eden blew out a breath. With the grand opening only days away, her doubts multiplied like yeast dough. Starting a new business was always risky. Did she have what it took to make hers a success?

Mary Jo frowned. "You're not worried, are you?"

"A little. Mostly I'm amazed it's all come together. Somewhere between the second and third coats of paint, I wasn't too sure."

Joe chuckled. "Or in the middle of laying the flooring."

"Yeah, there were a few moments when I had some serious doubts." Her gaze swept the room. "When I look around, I'm humbled you both have so much faith in me. I'm thankful to God for loving me enough to bring me and Jake here."

Mary Jo teared up. "You're a very easy person to love."

Eden wrapped her in a hug. "So are you."

Joe made gagging sounds. "Come on, Jake. While the girls are doing the mushy thing, you and I are going to the kitchen to see the really cool stuff."

Jake giggled. "Cool."

"Wait for us." Mary Jo released Eden with a laugh. "We don't want to miss the cool stuff."

While Eden was proud of the front of the shop, she was awed by the kitchen. The public half of the bakery was a welcoming haven of soft colors and interesting textiles. The kitchen was all business.

A massive state-of-the-art oven had pride of place along the far wall and was flanked by two gleaming towers of stainless cooling racks. On the opposite side, they'd installed an oversized double sink and an industrial capacity dishwasher to handle cleanup. A huge stainless-topped worktable ran through the center of the room.

"My goodness, look at the size of this table," Mary Jo's eyes widened. "It must be ten feet long."

"Twelve and a half." Eden pointed to her partner. "Joe designed and built it."

The older woman nodded in his direction. "You certainly have a gift."

Eden smiled. "I'm telling you, the man's a genius. He wired it to handle my mixers. And he also came up with the idea of building the shelf under it. This way I can store my bowls and pans and stuff underneath so they'll always be accessible."

He looked pleased but embarrassed by the praise. "We wanted the table to serve as control central. With the sink here and the oven there, everything she needs is within easy reach."

Mary Jo pointed to a second corral in the corner. "I see Jake has a play area in here as well."

"It won't work forever, but for now he's content to hang out in there as long as he can see me."

"Anytime he wants out, he can stay with me." Mary Jo smiled. "Remember, I'm always available to babysit."

"You can be sure we'll be calling you, but you're a busy woman with a life of your own. Once Jake and I move in upstairs, *if* Jake and I move in upstairs, it'll be simpler to keep him here with me."

Joe cleared his throat. "Speaking of the upstairs, do you want to check it out?"

Eden saw a look pass between him and Mary Jo. Secrets? "Has the inspector finally cleared it?"

He nodded. "As a matter of fact, he did. And you'll be happy to know everything passed with flying colors."

She thought of the ancient plumbing and appliances waiting up there. "Really? I wonder what took him so long."

Joe shrugged. "The city works in mysterious ways."

Joe opened the heavy door in the back of the kitchen that led to the flight of stairs up to the second-floor apartment.

Eden reached for Jake. "Here, why don't you let me carry him? You've been chasing him around all morning."

He tightened his grip on the toddler and turned slightly to deflect her outstretched arms. "He's no problem. You go ahead and lead the way. The door's unlocked."

They were halfway to the top when Eden stopped and looked back at him. "I know you did a lot of work on the stairway, but I honestly can't find the patches."

He grinned. "Virtually invisible, you might say."

She nodded and continued the climb and pushed open the door when she reached the apartment. "Somebody left the lights on in here."

The indignation in her voice brought a smile to his face. He'd learned early on a woman raised in straitened circumstances had no tolerance for waste. "It's okay. We'll get them when we leave."

He hurried up the remaining steps, Jake giggling with every bounce, so he could see her expression when she moved over the threshold.

She took three steps inside, stopped, and pressed her hands to her cheeks. "What's going on?" She whirled around to face him. "What is this?"

He lifted his shoulders in a careless shrug, as if he hadn't poured heart and soul into making it perfect for her. "Mary Jo and I fixed up the place for you and Jake."

Her gaze rested a moment on his, touched on Mary Jo's, then turned back to the room. "It's incredible."

She pushed open the door to the tiny bathroom off the kitchen and flipped on the light. "It's beautiful."

He snorted. "It's a toilet."

"It's a beautiful toilet. And a beautiful sink. And a beautiful mirror."

"So you like it?"

"I love it. It's—"

"—beautiful, yeah, we got that."

She stood transfixed in the doorway of the room no bigger than a closet, her hands flattened over her heart.

After a minute or two, Joe tapped her on the shoulder. "Come on, Florida. Enough with the bathroom, already. We've got a whole apartment to see."

She turned, her expression dazed. "I know, but it's just so . . . beautiful."

He laughed. "If you're this excited about a toilet, I can't wait to see your reaction to the washer and dryer."

Her blue gaze raised to his, and a joy he would never forget spread across her face. "I have my own washer and dryer?"

"Yes, ma'am." He walked her the four short steps to the laundry room and pushed open the sliding door.

It took her at least five minutes to inspect the machines, squealing her delight over the luxury of having her very own appliances. "Do you see this, Jake? We've got a washer and dryer."

Jake was not impressed. Neither was he enamored of the double sink, the stove with a glass top range, or the refrigerator, although his mother extolled the virtues of each item at some length. He perked up at the sight of the cookie jar Mary Jo had thoughtfully filled with the animal crackers she knew he enjoyed. He accepted her invitation to sit with her at the kitchen table for a snack while his mother and Joe continued the tour.

They'd only progressed a few feet, just past the table and the wall that separated the kitchen from the L-shaped living area, when Eden stopped again.

"It's perfect." She turned to Joe, a question on her face. "How did you know?"

"How did I know what?"

She swept her arm in a broad arc, indicating the entire room. "Everything. The colors, the shape of the sofas, the pillows, the rug. How did you know *exactly* what I wanted?"

He cocked a thumb toward the kitchen. "Can't take the credit. I'm just the labor. Mary Jo was your decorator."

Eden turned to Mary Jo. "It's like you looked inside my head and saw everything just as I imagined it." She chuckled. "And then upgraded it about 1,000 percent."

Mary Jo smiled. "You must have noticed I've asked quite a few pointed questions about how you planned to decorate once you moved in. I told Joe I was afraid all our discussions might lead you to suspect something and spoil the surprise."

"I had no clue." Eden shook her head. "I don't know when or how you did it all. How did you even get in here when the city inspector wouldn't sign off on the stairs?"

Joe cleared his throat. "I may not have been entirely truthful with you about the whole inspection thing. There was never anything wrong with the stairs."

Hands on hips, she narrowed her eyes at him. "You lied to me?"

He lifted his palms. "Only a little. And for a very good cause. You have no idea how hard it's been to keep all this from you."

Mary Jo laughed. "We've been positively devious, sneaking around day and night. Well, just the day for me."

Eden's eyes snapped back to his. "You've been working on the apartment at night?"

He nodded. "Pretty much solid for the last few weeks."

"What about the harem?"

He laughed. "No time for anything but building if we were going to get you in here before the grand opening." He saw a tear slide down her cheek, and his heart sank. "What's the matter?"

She sniffled. "You and Mary Jo went to all this trouble for Jake and me?"

Mary Jo got up from the table and crossed the room to take Eden's hands. "It was a labor of love, dear one. We're so proud of you and all you've done. We want you and Jake to have a cozy place to call home."

"You two are the absolute best." He could hear tears in her voice as she hugged Mary Jo. "I love you."

"I love you too."

"Nuh-uh, ladies." He waved his hands in warning. "No way we're sidetracking down mushy stuff lane. We've still got two bedrooms and a bathroom left to go."

Eden gave a teary laugh as they split apart. "The man hasn't got a sentimental bone in his body."

"More to the point, I have business in Fort Worth this afternoon." It was true. Fact was, he had no reason to be here for the unveiling of the apartment. Mary Jo knew the place as well as he did. She could have shown Eden around, but he wouldn't have missed seeing the look on her face when she first saw it for anything in the world.

Eden was all about home and family. Whether because of her upbringing or being a single mother, providing a good place to raise her son was priority one. He admired her for it.

Building out the bakery, they'd had a lot of time to talk. Somewhere in the long hours of construction, they'd developed the habit of turning down the radio so they could visit while they worked. It didn't take long to discover the woman had strong opinions about what it took to create a warm, nurturing environment.

So he listened and took mental notes of the things she wanted. One night after supper, when he and Mary Jo had the opportunity to speak privately, he mentioned wanting to spruce up the apartment. Seemed Mary Jo had been thinking along the same lines, and over the kitchen table that night, the plan was born. They would secretly refurbish the old place and present her with a move-in ready home.

What started as a good deed for a worthy cause quickly spiraled into a near obsession. It got so bad, he'd begun counting the hours until he could get back here to work. The time he'd spent scraping up old linoleum and retexturing walls, tasks he normally despised, seemed to fly by, so great was his desire to build Eden and Jake the place of their dreams.

Mary Jo reseated herself at the table, and Jake crawled up in her lap. "Why don't you and Eden look around while Jake and I finish the cookies?"

"Good plan." He extended an arm toward Eden. "Shall we?"

He knew he'd struck gold in the full bathroom by the look of wonder on her face when she stepped inside, though for the life of him he couldn't figure out who Andy and Bee were or why they'd be so pleased with the updates. She loved every inch of it, and that's what mattered to him.

As they walked through the connecting door to the primary bedroom, he locked onto her expression, awaiting her reaction.

He heard her breath catch.

"It's a princess room," she whispered.

Knowing how much she loved the room she occupied at Mary Jo's, they'd recreated the space for Eden here. The four-poster bed, though not antique, was the same basic style and color, and they'd dressed it in pure white bedding and a mound of pillows worthy of royalty.

She moved slowly, almost reverently, through the high-ceilinged room, stroking a hand over the comforter, the lace of a pillow, the carved poster of the bed. She crossed to the windows, rubbing the rich drapery fabric between her fingers as she peered through the panes.

"It's perfect."

He didn't like the sudden seriousness of her tone. "Not quite. The closet's still a joke."

She walked to it and peeked in. "It's perfect to me."

"You're an easy sell."

She followed him into the hall and down to Jake's room. She paused just outside the doorway, calling over her shoulder, "Jake, come see your new room."

He toddled in, Mary Jo trailing him, and made a beeline for the giant black teddy bear propped against a bookcase painted in the same cheery red as the crib and chest of drawers. "Mine."

"Yeah, little dude, it's all yours. You hit the jackpot, my man."

Eden gave Joe a look of bewilderment. "Where did all these toys and books come from?"

"The internet." He stuffed his hands in his pockets and shrugged. "Okay, I may have gotten a little carried away, but a kid needs some stuff."

Her gaze swept the room. "He's certainly got some now."

The undercurrent of seriousness was still there, and he was almost afraid to ask her opinion. "So, what do you think?"

She took a deep breath before meeting his eyes. "I think Jake and I are the luckiest people in the world. I think you and Mary Jo are the most generous people I've ever known, and I think I'm going to cry." With that, she buried her face in her hands and sobbed.

Mary Jo and he exchanged a look of alarm. Ordinarily unmoved by a woman's tears, seeing Eden cry went straight to his heart.

He stepped toward her. "Are those happy or sad tears?"

She lifted her face, amazingly beautiful even with red splotches, and nodded.

"Which?"

"Both."

That did it. He closed the distance between them and wrapped his arms around her. She stiffened, probably in shock that her partner was manhandling her, but she didn't pull away.

Jake looked up from the truck he was pushing along the floor. "Mama?" He trundled over to her. "My mama," he repeated, wrapping his arms around her leg.

Joe reached down and stroked a hand over his head. "It's okay, little man. I'm not trying to take her. I just don't want her to be sad."

She swiped the back of her hand across her eyes and stepped out of the circle of his arms. "I'm not sad, exactly." She scooped up her son and hugged him to her chest. "The apartment is beautiful, more than I could ever have imagined, and I know Jake and I will be so happy here."

She paused to draw a steadying breath. "But I realize that when we move in, everything will change." She took another deep inhalation. "These last six weeks, living with Mary Jo, have been the best of my life. This will sound silly, but I felt like we were a family. I couldn't have asked for a better mother than Mary Jo, and Jake . . ." She stopped as tears choked off the words.

Mary Jo laid one hand on Eden's back and the other on Joe's arm, linking them together. "We *are* a family. You and Jake are mine, just as much as my precious Joseph. God brought you all to me, and I intend to keep you, no matter where you live."

Eden smiled through a sheen of moisture. "I'm so glad. I know we'll get together—"

"I'm already counting on you for Saturday night slumber parties."

"And you and Jake will come to dinner," Joe added.

Eden brushed away a leaking tear. "Yes, we will. I'm just being emotional and silly. Blame it on nerves about opening the bakery and shock over my amazing apartment."

Mary Jo kept her hands resting on each of them. "Honestly, I think it's Joe who'll have the biggest adjustment. His every waking hour for the last month and a half has been dedicated to building the bakery and apartment. Now that it's complete, he's going to have a lot of time on his hands."

Eden smiled up at him. "I bet it's a relief to get your life back."

"Oh yeah, sure," he lied. "And if I need a dose of the dude here, I can hang out with you two some evenings."

She brightened, apparently pleased with the idea, but Mary Jo shook her head.

"You won't be able to hang out here."

Both Eden and Joe turned to stare at her. "Why not?"

She frowned as she dropped her arms. "Let's face it. We have a lot of small-minded citizens in our little community. Thanks to one particularly small mind, people were given the erroneous impression that our Eden is less than a virtuous woman."

"Marilyn." He still saw red when he thought about the rumors she'd started.

Mary Jo nodded. "I feel we've done well disseminating the truth about Eden and Jake, but the damage was already done. As a new business owner, dependent on the good will of the locals, Eden will have to be particularly vigilant in maintaining a spotless reputation."

"That's ridiculous. It's not right. It's not fair." Even as he said it, he knew Mary Jo was correct.

Her smile dimmed as she shook her head. "No, it's not fair. Life rarely is. However, the fact remains, the sight of your truck parked at her building is sure to stir up talk. To protect Eden and her reputation, you'll have to stay away."

Pfft. Pfft. Pfft. One by one he could hear his fantasies deflate.

Like the one he had about him, Eden and Jake sitting around the little kitchen table, enjoying a meal together, like a family. Pfft.

Or the fantasy he'd woven as he carried the rocking chair into Jake's room and set it by the toy chest. The one where he'd read Jake a story before he and Eden tucked him in for the night. Pfft.

Or his favorite, the one in which he and Eden watched a movie, snuggled together on the couch, after they'd tucked Jake into bed. Pfft.

Seemed Eden was on to something. There was plenty to be sad about after all.

Pfft.

CHAPTER TWELVE

Sunlight flooded through the arched, stained-glass windows, painting the pew and floor beneath it with shimmering patches of rich color. Each Sunday, Eden liked to imagine the brilliant show was all for her, a secret message from her heavenly Father, like a wink, reminding her how much He loved her and how very proud He was to call her His child.

She had so much to be thankful for. Her heart swelled with gratitude, and she whispered, "Thank you."

"Hmm?" Joe ducked his head toward hers. Though they were the only occupants on the pew, they sat hip to hip. "You say something?"

"Nuh-uh." Over the weeks since her salvation, she'd shared the details of her journey with Joe. Partially because it was so nice to talk about her experiences, but more because she wanted him to join her.

In conversations with Mary Jo, she'd gained the impression Joe had once walked with God, but over time had drifted away. Eden knew he was saved—she'd asked him point blank—but it was clear his faith had taken a back seat to the other demands in his life.

Eden wanted better for him. She wanted him to have the joy she had, to know the sense of security she'd found. So she discussed spiritual things with him while they worked on the bakery.

But even so, she wouldn't tell him about the sunbeams. That was private, just between her and her Father.

The service hadn't started yet. People were still entering the sanctuary and finding seats. Mary Jo had yet to join them. She liked to buzz around the room, like a bee flitting from flower to flower, catching up with friends until the organ started playing.

Joe leaned close, his breath moving the hair by her ear when he whispered, "I thought the nursery lady was less horrible today. She actually smiled at Jake and almost looked you in the eye when you spoke to her." He nudged her. "I think you're making progress, Florida."

Eden chuckled. "It's got to be the prayer."

"You're praying for the mean nursery lady?"

"Yup. The Bible says we have to pray for our enemies. So I pray for her. And Marilyn too." She'd tried to pray for Eunice Welts, but so far every time she brought the old gossip to mind, she got angry. For now, she was asking God to help her *want* to pray for Eunice.

Baby steps, Mary Jo called them.

"Good girl. We need to be all prayed up for the grand opening tomorrow."

She felt a hitch of nerves. "You're praying too. Right?"

He placed a hand over hers and gave it a squeeze. "Absolutely. And as we know, the effective, fervent prayer of the righteous man avails much."

She shifted so she could smile up into his handsome face. "Give the man a gold star."

Mary Jo had tasked her with memorizing a new scripture each week, and Eden turned around and assigned the same memory verse to Joe. They'd made it a contest, to see who could be first to recite it correctly. They'd laughed a lot, and more importantly, they'd already learned a half a dozen verses.

"I'm thinking about making tacos for dinner at Mary Jo's tonight. That work for you?"

Eden shook her head. "Jake and I aren't going to make it. In case you haven't heard, I'm opening a bakery tomorrow, so I thought maybe I should stay home and bake something."

"Okay. After we're done with dinner, I'll run by and give you a hand."

She frowned. "No, you better not."

"You're not still worried about gossip, are you?"

She nodded. "We've put so much into the bakery. It'd be a shame to undo all our hard work this close to opening."

He draped an arm across the back of the pew, his hand resting on her shoulder in a gesture of solidarity. "It's stupid. We're in business together, for heaven's sake. I don't know why people can't see we're just friends."

Since their hug in her apartment the other day, a comforting gesture when she needed it, their relationship had undergone a subtle change. They touched.

They hugged, and even kissed goodbye, if you considered a brief peck on the cheek a kiss.

Prior to their embrace in the apartment, they'd kept a wary distance from one another. There'd been a hundred times she'd wanted to hug him, like when he said or did something funny, or sometimes just because he was an amazing guy, but she'd held back. She didn't know the precise etiquette for business associates, but she was pretty sure it was keep-your-hands-to-yourself.

Somewhere over the weeks of hard work and enforced togetherness, they'd gone beyond the bounds of business partners into the realm of friends. Good friends. She'd told him things she'd never told a soul, and she knew he'd done the same with her.

They "got" each other, which was why the new physical connection would never be a problem. Neither of them had any interest in romance. Joe had his harem, and she had Jesus and Jake.

In their own way, each was complete. Satisfied.

Eden glanced at the baby monitor perched on the corner of the prep table. Jake was still moving around in his crib, the last few wiggles before he drifted off to sleep. The microphone in the device picked up his baby chatter, mostly gibberish, punctuated with the occasional recognizable word or name. Right now he was talking about Joe.

The depth of the bond between them still surprised her. Jake fell hard and fast for Joe. Just the sound of his voice was enough to light up her son's face. The shocking thing was watching tough guy Joe fall for Jake. It hadn't happened overnight, but once he warmed up to her son, he was Jake's biggest fan.

Smiling, she directed her attention to the sheet of pastry she'd rolled out. She pressed a round cutter into the still cool dough, lifted it over the waiting tart pan, and gently released the disk into the indentation. She worked quickly, before the dough warmed up and grew sticky, cutting out rounds and fitting them into the pan. When she'd cut out all she could, she combined the remaining pastry into a ball, rolled it out, and repeated the process.

The buzzer on the oven sounded. She picked up a pot holder, pulled open the oven door, and removed two pans of tart shells. She added the fragrant, golden-brown crusts to the others already cooling on the rack and slid the waiting pans into the oven. After setting the timer, she carried the bowl and utensils to the sink for a quick rinse, then into the dishwasher.

A peek at the monitor told her Jake was finally asleep. She sighed, taking a moment to stretch out the kinks in her spine before starting the icing for the cupcakes. What a blessing that she was here, working in the bakery on tomorrow's goodies while her son slept in his own room one story above her. Mary Jo spoke often about God going beyond all they could ask or think. This was surely a prime example.

When she'd loaded Jake and all their worldly belongings into her car two short months ago, she was determined to build a good life for them. The best she'd hoped for was a small apartment and a job to pay for it. Definitely no frills.

Instead, here she was in her very own bakery, below the spacious, fully furnished apartment she and her son occupied free of charge. Miraculous.

She should be the happiest, most grateful woman in the world. And she was . . .

How could she not be when God had given her everything she'd dreamed of? He'd provided a job and a home so she and Jake could live as a family. Beyond that, He'd given her Jesus and called her into *His* family. She had everything she'd thought she needed to be complete.

She didn't know where the loneliness came from. When it cropped up as she and Jake sat at their dinner table for the first time, she told herself it was just a matter of adjustment. They'd grown accustomed to sharing meals with Mary Jo and Joe, and it would take a while to acclimate to being a family of two.

The unsettled feelings retreated, like a shadow in the light, only to resurface at Jake's bath. Normally the hour before bed was the happiest time of day, but lately she couldn't help but feel it would be so much sweeter with someone to share it.

She smiled at the memory of Jake's belly laughs when Joe took over bath time at Mary Jo's. The two of them staged boat races, did bubble sculpting, and generally made a mess of the floor. Joe's presence made a good time better.

Even here, in the midst of her beautiful workroom, built to her specifications and outfitted with the best of everything, something was missing.

Make that someone.

Joe had spent as much time in here as she had, and somewhere along the line she'd begun to associate him with the space, so much that when he wasn't here it felt wrong. Empty.

After the new oven arrived and she'd had to experiment with cooking temperatures and load size, he'd willingly sat here for hours, keeping her company while she baked. Besides being her business partner and building contractor, he'd served as an enthusiastic taste tester, sounding board, and all-around handyman.

She didn't know when she'd become so dependent on him for her happiness. It would take a week or so before she found her equilibrium, and everything returned to normal.

She plopped down on the stool, sunk her chin in her hands, and sighed. Who was she kidding? A week, a month, even a year from now wouldn't make any difference. There wouldn't be any normal without the man she loved.

Okay, she'd finally admitted it. She was in love with Joe. How an intelligent woman thoroughly opposed to romance should find herself in this position didn't matter. She was too much a realist to ignore so obvious a truth.

She loved him.

After her fiasco attempt to build a family of her own, she'd denied herself the possibility of finding a mate. She and Jake were rocking along just fine. They didn't need anything or anyone.

Maybe she'd been too hasty.

While she didn't need a man to survive, the right one could bring so much richness to her life. And Jake's. Of course, it would take a special man to complete her little family. He'd have to be a believer, certainly. He'd have to be a man of integrity, hardworking, and compassionate. A sense of humor was a must.

And though she wanted a physical attraction, tingles preferred but not essential, she realized she could never be drawn to a man, no matter how attractive, who didn't love her son. Jake was part of her—a package deal.

She ticked the essential qualities off her fingers. So far, Joe met every criteria. Exceeded them.

But there was one more. He'd have to want her exclusively.

As in, no harems.

She bowed her head over the soon-to-be-iced lemon cupcakes. "Father, thank You for all of this." She paused as a swell of gratitude rolled over her. "You've given me so much, and if You don't want to do another thing for me, I totally understand. But I love him. I didn't mean to fall for him, but I did. So, although You've already blessed me with so much, I'd like to add Joe to the mix. Can I have Jesus, Jake, *and* Joe?"

Joe gave the ingredients in the pan a final stir. "Dinner will be ready in five minutes."

"Umm, that smells delicious." Mary Jo peeked around his shoulder. "Mercy! You must be starving."

He laughed as he turned off the heat under a pan of enough taco meat to feed a family of eight. "It'll take me a while to remember how to cook for just the two of us."

She sighed. "I miss them."

"Me too. It's too quiet. And tidy. I almost scattered plastic bowls and lids on the floor when I got here just because it doesn't feel right not to step over them while I cook."

Mary Jo nodded. "I catch myself looking into Eden's room a half dozen times a day, waiting for Jake's dear little face to pop around the corner."

He wrapped an arm around her shoulders. "We're a pretty pitiful pair."

The doorbell chimed and delight lit Mary Jo's face. "Maybe that's them."

He scrambled down the hall, Mary Jo at his heels. She opened the door, and her smile faltered. "Oh, Todd. Hello. We weren't expecting you."

"Hello, Mary Jo." Her nephew, sixtyish, with heavy jowls and a receding hairline, looked at Joe and frowned. "I see you're still hanging around. You're a grown man, now. Don't you think you should have a place of your own?"

Mary Joe held the door for him to enter. "Tsk, Todd. Joe has a lovely home."

"Which he can no doubt afford by sponging off of you."

Joe directed his comment to Mary Jo's ear and pitched it just above a whisper. "Says the man who always manages to show up at mealtime."

She shushed him before turning back to Todd. "We were just about to sit down to dinner. Do you have time to join us?"

"I'd be happy to." He glared at Joe. "I've been meaning to stop by for a while, but I'm a very busy man."

"Busy*body*," Joe corrected.

"Joseph." She lifted a brow in warning as she directed her nephew toward the kitchen. "Come sit down, and I'll set a place for you."

She gathered a plate, silverware, and a napkin and placed them on the table while Todd lowered his bulk into the chair.

Joe delivered the serving bowls to the table and sat. He waited until after Mary Jo was seated and said the blessing to ask him, "To what do we owe the, uh, pleasure of your company this evening?"

Todd picked up the bowl of taco meat and spooned a mound on his plate. "I'm here to visit *Mary Jo* because a mutual friend of ours mentioned a very unsuitable house guest is staying here."

Joe wrinkled his forehead in feigned misunderstanding. "Doesn't sound like any friend of mine."

"Eunice Welts must have called you." Mary Jo's face creased with displeasure.

"Yes, she did." He picked up a tortilla and made a taco. "And you should be thankful to have friends looking out for you. Honestly, Mary Jo, what are you thinking, opening your home to some loose woman and her—"

"—you don't want to call her that." Joe glared at the self-righteous old windbag.

"Certainly, I do." He must have gotten a good look at the fury on Joe's face. He cleared his throat. "Er, the point is, this is one more example of people taking advantage of you. I've had my doubts about a woman your age living here alone and unprotected—"

"—I'm neither alone nor unprotected." She reached her hand across the table to pat Joe's. "I have my Joe."

It looked as though Todd would have liked to argue, but after darting a glance at Joe, he seemed to change his mind. "Nonetheless, opening your home to a stranger puts your mental competence in question."

"Mary Jo's company did not sit down to the dinner table before we had a police report on her guest."

Both Mary Jo and Todd looked at him in surprise.

"Well, I must say, that showed some presence of mind." Todd stuffed an oversized bite of taco into his mouth. "That doesn't negate the fact she took advantage of your good nature."

She shook her head. "She didn't take advantage of me. She asked to pay me."

"Are you saying you collected rent from the woman?"

"What she's saying is that her company wasn't the type to accept charity." Joe directed a quelling look at Mary Jo that said *leave it alone.*

Todd rocked back in his chair to study her. "Well, well. That's better. Well done, Mary Jo." He placed an enormous scoop of guacamole on his plate to replace the one he'd polished off. "So where is the, uh, young woman now? I confess I'm curious to see her."

"She's not here," Mary Jo said. "She has her own apartment."

"She's staying in town?"

Joe smirked. "Seems your source isn't doing a very good job of keeping you up to date."

"She's opening a bakery," Mary Jo said.

"She's a businesswoman?"

Joe nodded. "And a darling of the mayor and chamber of commerce. Think how well it reflects on Mary Jo to have been the first to welcome her to town."

The look Todd focused on Mary Jo was something akin to wonder. "I'll say it again. Well done."

The rest of dinner passed without incident, probably because Joe decided to follow the old adage "If you don't have something nice to say, don't say anything at all." Todd didn't require a partner for conversation; in fact, he seemed happiest when he had the floor all to himself. He complained uninterrupted about his family, his job, and the state of the world while stuffing his face full of food.

As soon as they finished eating and Todd put down his napkin, Joe pushed his chair back and stood. "This has been great. Thanks for coming."

"My overnight bag is in the car—"

Joe helped Todd to his feet and unceremoniously herded him toward the entrance, Mary Jo practically running behind them to catch up. "Good thing you didn't bring it in. Mary Jo's got a commitment with the mayor tonight, no telling when she'll be through."

"But—"

Joe swung open the door. "As busy as Mary Jo is, it'd be a good idea if you call before you come next time, and she can try to pencil you in."

"Well, I—" Todd stepped over the threshold.

Mary Jo stood at his side while Joe waved her nephew off. "Thanks again. Goodnight."

He waited until Todd crossed the porch and started down the stairs before shutting the door.

She turned a dazed look up at him. "Mercy, Joseph."

He gave her an innocently bland look. "What? I thought that went very well."

She shook her head. "I'm not sure what to think. The things you said to him . . ." She blinked. "What would Matthew say about all those lies?"

"What lies?"

Mary Jo could look fierce if she wanted to. She balled her fists and propped them on her hips. "You told him we had a police report on Eden."

He met her gaze squarely. "We did."

Her blue eyes went wide after searching his face for the truth. "Joseph Wolfe, I don't even know what to say to that." She pointed an accusing finger at him. "What about telling him I collected rent from Eden?"

"If you recall, I never said those words. I can't help it if the old money grubber inferred it from my remarks."

She wagged her head. "Okay, Mr. Slippery, what about telling him I had a commitment with the mayor this evening?"

He shrugged. "You do. You told him you'd give him a call tonight and let him know if you needed a ride to the ribbon cutting tomorrow. That's a commitment."

She let her arms fall to her sides in defeat. "I can't feel comfortable misleading him. As much as he annoys me, he's still my nephew."

"Then let me take care of him. Because I've got no problem with it." Joe gently took hold of her shoulders and looked into her face. "You and I both know he came here tonight to make trouble. I'm tired of his harping about your mental competency."

She wrapped her arms around his waist for a quick hug. "What a blessing to have such a fierce protector by my side."

"I'm happy to do it. Now come on back to the kitchen." He turned and started down the hall. "I'll clear the table, and we can have some of the cake Eden sent."

She stopped short. "We had dessert, and you didn't offer any to Todd?"

Uh-oh. Trading insults was one thing, but withholding dessert from a guest was going too far. He'd clearly offended her deeply ingrained hostess sensibilities. He faced her. "Anybody who bad-mouths our Eden doesn't deserve any of her cake."

She seemed to weigh the argument before nodding. "You're right."

Harmony restored, they walked side by side to the kitchen. She carried the dirty dishes to the sink where he rinsed them and placed them in the dishwasher. Once the table was clean, he cut them each a slice of strawberry layer cake and delivered them to the table.

Mary Jo forked off a bite. "Funny, tonight started out with you and I complaining about how lonely it would be at dinner."

He nodded. "Todd's visit should serve as a warning to us. Be careful what you wish for."

"I feel sorry for him." She sighed. "To hear him talk, he must be miserable. I've never heard him say a positive thing about his job or his family."

Joe poked at the pink icing with his fork. "Have you ever thought of me as a family man?"

She put down her fork to give him her full attention. "I beg your pardon?"

"You know, a guy with a wife and kids."

She chuckled. "I'm familiar with the concept. As to ever having thought of you as a family man? No. But only because you've told me a million times you'll never marry."

"Suppose I told you I was thinking about it now?"

She stilled as the weight of his words sank in. Her expression softened, and tears filled her eyes. "Really? You'd be a wonderful husband and father, Joe. The very best."

Some of the tension between his shoulders eased. "What about my past? Eden says it doesn't matter, but my gene pool isn't much to brag about."

"Your father was dreadful, certainly, but your mother may have been very nice. She must have been beautiful. You got your good looks somewhere, and it wasn't your father."

He cut off the corner of his cake, raised it to his mouth. "I've always thought she got off easy when she left. But something Eden said has stuck in my mind. She said there was no crueler punishment than to deprive a woman of her child."

"I'm sure Eden's right."

"Doesn't it seem to you that if my mother were truly worried about me, she'd have tried to see me, to check and be sure I was okay?"

"Yes, it does. But we don't know her circumstances. Maybe she couldn't come. We don't know if she's still alive."

"She'd have to be relatively young. Midfifties, I'd think."

"Have you ever thought about looking for her?"

He shook his head. "I'd pretty much written her off until Eden pointed out how difficult it would have been for her to leave. Since then I've been curious, but it's probably a chapter better left closed." He scooped up another bite of cake. "So what do you think? I need you to be honest. With all my baggage, am I crazy to think I could have a family of my own?"

She smiled. "Not crazy. Hopeful. It shows you're a man of faith who believes God's promises when He says you are a new creation."

"I do believe that, it's just my past—"

She held up a palm. "—is passed. Obviously it plays some part in shaping you into the man you've become, but remember, your father wasn't the only influence in your life. I recall a childless couple who loved you as their own son and did everything in their power to ensure you grew up into a fine young man who knew right from wrong."

Now *he* teared up as a million memories flooded in. He smiled at her. "I remember them. Nice people but relentless. They fed me, clothed me, and educated me. They made me say 'yes ma'am' and 'yes sir,' and change my socks, and dragged me to church every Sunday whether I wanted to go or not."

She grinned. "They were tough."

"They were awesome." He took her hand. "And if I haven't thanked you recently, let me say how very grateful I am to have had you and Matthew in my life. You were the best parents a guy could ask for."

She covered his hand with her free one. "And you were the very best son." She lifted her hand to smack his. "So make a mother's joy complete and marry Eden and Jake so I can be a grandma."

"You think she'd have me?" Doubts continued to circle. "She's not too keen on marriage."

"Then you'll have to change her mind." She picked up her fork. "And Joe dear, my money's on you."

CHAPTER THIRTEEN

Eden had already put in two hours downstairs when Joe and Mary Jo arrived at seven the next day. She stood behind the service counter, artfully arranging cupcakes on cake stands when she saw them through the glass.

Joe unlocked the door, and the little bell chimed when they stepped inside. "Good morning! Ready for the big day?"

"Yes and no." She felt as she did after studying for an exam—woefully unprepared in spite of massive preparation and yet eager to get past the nerves and just plunge in.

She met them in front of the counter and hugged them both. "Wow, I feel better already."

Joe kept an arm around her shoulders. "Mary Jo and me. Good medicine."

Mary Jo glanced around. "Is Jake up yet?"

Eden pulled the monitor from her back pocket. "Just stirring."

"I can go up and wait for him. He and I will have breakfast and be down and dressed before the ribbon cutting."

Eden sighed. "Thank you, Mary Jo. You're a lifesaver."

"Put me to work." Joe glanced hopefully toward the gleaming stainless machines behind the counter. "Do you want me to start the coffee and tea?"

"Already started." She shrugged at his look of surprise. "I woke up early and couldn't go back to sleep, so I've been down here doing the last-minute stuff."

"Nervous?" Mary Jo asked.

She bobbed her head. "A little."

"Let's have a quick prayer before I head upstairs." They linked hands and Mary Jo prayed. "Mighty One, we are awed by Your goodness to us. Thank You for this beautiful bakery. We invite Your presence here and ask You to bless every part of the day. Amen."

She gave their hands a squeeze before releasing them. "I'll see you two in an hour or so. Call if you need something."

Eden intercepted a look between them before Mary Jo walked out. "What was that?"

"Nothing." A self-conscious look flashed across his face. "She's probably warning me not to eat the inventory before we open."

Eden snorted. "Good luck with that. I've got enough to stock every bakery in Texas. I got pretty carried away, but I have no idea how many people to expect."

"Tough call. I mean, if every man, woman, and child from this bustling metropolis came through the door, we'd have a whopping five hundred customers."

"Oh, Joe." Sudden panic rushed in as the last six weeks of her life flashed before her eyes, highlighting every sweaty, exhausting minute it took to arrive where they were today. "Are we insane? Spending all this time and money to build a big, beautiful business in the middle of nowhere? Is this crazy?"

He wrapped a strong arm around her shoulders and guided her back to the workroom. "Crazy is such an ugly word. I prefer to think of us as visionaries."

She laughed as she lifted her face to his. "Thank you." She pressed a kiss to his freshly shaven cheek.

"For what?"

"For partnering with me. For sharing my vision."

He gave her braid a quick tug. "Aw, Florida, we're going to make an unstoppable team."

The look he gave her, a potent combination of admiration and tenderness, sent her heart racing. She could have read it wrong, but it seemed to suggest the team he was talking about didn't end at the front door of the bakery.

Maybe her prayer for the whole package wasn't as ridiculous as she'd feared.

Joe glanced at his watch. "We've got forty-seven minutes until showtime. What do you need me to do?"

"I've got a pan of cinnamon rolls ready to be iced."

"If the job includes samples, I'm your man." He looked toward the oven and sniffed. "Do I smell more baking?"

She grinned. "You're good. I made an extra pan to feed the mayor and whoever represents the city at the ribbon cutting."

While Joe smeared cream cheese icing on the rolls, Eden ferried goodies from the racks in the workroom to the glass-fronted counter and arranged everything by type. The individually wrapped iced cookies she'd crafted with the Paradise logo went in a basket at the end of the service counter. Between the basket and the cash register at the other end, she mounded like items together. Cinnamon rolls, blueberry scones, banana muffins, tarts, three flavors of cupcakes, and fudgy, iced brownies that were as beautiful as they were decadent lined the granite surface.

In addition, she had four-layer cakes, two strawberry and two chocolate, in the glass-doored refrigerator facing the serving line.

Joe joined her when she stepped in front of the counter to survey the goods.

She frowned. "I should have made chocolate chip cookies."

"Are you kidding? This is great."

"Someone's going to want chocolate chip cookies—"

"Then they'll just have to come back." He placed his hands on her shoulders and gently turned her to face him. "You've thought long and hard about your inventory—"

She lifted her gaze to his. "You mean I obsessed."

He tilted his head as if considering, then grinned. "Well, yes, that word did come to mind. The point is you've got a great lineup. You were the one who told me we're in uncharted waters, and until you've got a week or two under your belt, we won't really know the best items to stock. For now, you've got something for everyone. Major crowd pleasers."

"What if we don't have a crowd?" Fear pressed the air from her chest. "What if no one comes?"

"Relax. Worst case scenario, you've got Mary Jo and whoever else from the chamber of commerce is willing to get out of bed for an 8:00 a.m. ribbon cutting. I know for a fact Hallie will be here, and lots of Mary Jo's church lady friends promised to come. You'll have a respectable showing."

She huffed out a breath. "You're right. I'm making myself crazy worrying about things I can't control."

"Opening day jitters." He pressed a quick kiss to her forehead before releasing her. "You're entitled."

"I just want it to be perfect. Speaking of which, would you be willing to man the cash register? I know I told you I could handle it all myself, but I'd feel better if you were back there with me today. I need the moral support."

A grin split his face. "I'm glad you asked because I'd already decided to hang out here for the day, making a nuisance of myself. If I'm behind the counter, I'll be less conspicuous. And while I'm back there, I think it only fair you let me be barista." He glanced at the equipment behind the counter. "The coffee machine is so cool." Of all the gadgets they'd acquired to start the business, Joe liked the coffee and tea machines the best.

"You know if you're serving coffee, you have to wear official Paradise Bakery clothing."

He looked toward the stack of neatly folded T-shirts on a shelf in the corner and grimaced. "Not the T-shirt."

She crossed her arms over her chest and nodded.

He shook his head. "I can't do it."

"Why not?" She glanced down at the one she wore under a crisp white apron embroidered with their logo. "What's wrong with the shirt?"

He screwed up his face as though it was painful to say. "It's . . . baby blue."

"So?"

"Guys do not wear baby blue."

"They do if they want to play barista."

He sighed. "Okay, fine." He sifted through the stack, checking the sizes, and slid one out from the middle. He held the offending garment in his right hand, well away from his body.

She made a show of looking at the clock. "We open in ten minutes. You'd better go ahead and put it on now."

"Yeah, yeah, I'm going." He was muttering something while he walked toward the workroom.

Eden would almost swear she heard him say, "the things we do for love," and was already heading in his direction to ask him to repeat it when she heard a tapping on the front door.

The mayor and several other older men stood outside, their faces pressed to the glass she'd spent an hour cleaning. She hurried to open the door before the logo on the window was obliterated by smudges. "Good morning." She waved them inside. "Thank you for coming."

"It smells great in here."

She smiled. "Once we have the ribbon cutting and pictures out of the way, I hope you'll stay for warm cinnamon rolls and coffee. My treat."

The ceremony went without a hitch. A dozen or so chamber of commerce members stood around on the sidewalk with Eden, Jake, Mary Jo, and Joe while the mayor gave a short speech about Paradise Bakery being the first of many new businesses the city would be welcoming as their plans for growth were realized. There was a slight delay when they discovered no one had thought to bring a pair of scissors, but a volunteered pocketknife from one of the assembled guests slit the length of red velvet ribbon they'd strung between two stanchions, and they were officially open.

Eden's friend Hallie snapped a few posed pictures of the group to post on social media and send to the county paper. After Pastor Dale closed with a prayer of blessing, they adjourned to the bakery for refreshments.

"Let me take Jake so you can do what you need to do," Mary Jo said. "I'll keep him down here as long as he's happy. If he gets fussy, I'll take him upstairs."

"Thank you." Eden transferred her willing son to Mary Jo before turning to Joe. "If you'll serve the coffee, I'll fix everyone a plate."

Hallie took a few pictures inside the shop, then tucked her camera in her purse. "Can I help?"

"That would be great." Eden led her into the workroom. "Two pairs of hands will make things move quicker."

"Everything looks amazing," Hallie said as they stood side by side, washing their hands at the sink. "The room out there is exactly what you described when you talked about your vision for the bakery."

"I tried to follow your advice and make sure everything here reinforces our brand."

"You nailed it."

"I can't take the credit." Eden dried her hands. "Any success here is a result of the hard work of so many people, including yours. Your marketing knowledge pushed us over the top."

Hallie sat on one of the stools. "I'm glad I could help. Of course, my motivation was totally selfish. By helping you get started in business here, I have a friend in town. And an extraordinary baker to create my wedding cake."

Eden picked up the tray of cinnamon rolls off the cooling rack and set it on the worktable next to the bowl of cream cheese icing. "What did Trey and your mom think about the sketches for the wedding cake?"

"They loved them."

"That's great." She glanced at the calendar hanging on the wall. "Wow, the wedding's coming up really quickly. Are you getting nervous?"

Hallie shook her head. "Impatient. I'm ready to be married."

"Makes sense. You've known each other a long time."

"That's true, but more than that, since we've gotten back together, he's become so important to me. It's hard to explain, but . . ." Her voice drifted off.

Eden nodded as she slathered icing on the still-warm rolls. "It's as if part of you is missing when you're not with him."

"Yes. Exactly. How did you—" Hallie's eyes went wide and her mouth formed an O. "You and Joe. I should have seen it sooner. It's written all over your face."

Eden lifted a hand to her cheek. "I hope it's not obvious."

Hallie frowned. "Why? It's great news. You two are perfect together."

"I don't know. It hit me so fast, and I'm not sure where he stands. Things have been crazy lately. There's been no time or energy to talk about us."

"Understandable. Maybe after today when things quiet down a bit—"

Eden looked up from separating the rolls with a spatula and placing them on plates. "You won't say anything, will you?"

"No way. But you'll keep me posted, right?"

"Absolutely. Friends keep friends in the loop."

Joe slid two large coffees across the counter. "Enjoy."

Mason Ryder picked up the cups. "You've done a nice job on this place. Really classy."

"Thank you. The credit goes to Eden. She's got a real knack for this kind of stuff."

Mrs. Ryder stepped up to gather their plated muffins. She glanced back at Eden, who talked with Sam at the end of the counter, before giving Joe a pointed look. "You two make a good team." The weight she'd placed on her words made more sense when she added, "It's past time you settled down and started a family."

Her husband grimaced. "Mercy, Jane! Lay off the matchmaking. Can't you see the man's trying to work?"

"I'm merely making polite conversation. Although it's as clear as the nose on your face they're crazy about each other. It just makes sense for them to get married and keep the business in the family."

Mason rolled his eyes. "Well, there you go, Joe. If you're looking for a reason to get hitched, the missus here has it all figured out for you. Marry the baker so you can simplify payroll."

Joe laughed. "Thank you, sir. I'll keep that in mind."

They headed off to an empty table when Sam approached. He looked Joe up and down and gave a low whistle. "Nice shirt, dude. Very pretty."

Joe glared at him. "Don't make me assault an officer." He filled an insulated cup with coffee, fitted it into a sleeve embossed with the Paradise logo and handed it to his friend. "What's up?"

Sam shot a glance over his shoulder at Eden. "Looking in on my girl. Now that she's settled, I figure it's time to try my hand at a little wooing."

Joe frowned and lowered his voice. "About that. Turns out she's not your girl." He cleared his throat. "She's mine."

"Wait." Sam put down his cup to lock eyes with him. "I thought you said you were leaving the playing field open to me. You know, all that talk about you not being interested."

Had he said that? What an idiot he'd been. "I'm sorry, bro. Plans change."

Sam straightened a fraction, a muscle twitching in his suddenly squared jaw. "She's not just another one of your women." His whisper was heated. "She's special."

Joe allowed his gaze to rest on her a moment. "Yeah, I got that."

Sam sighed and his expression softened. "I can see you do." He picked up his coffee. "I guess I can try one of those online dating sites. Or maybe someone from your black book."

Eden moved to Joe's side. "Everything okay? Sam, you look upset. Is something wrong?"

He sent a speaking glance to Joe before turning to her and shaking his head. "It's all good."

Her frown said she wasn't convinced.

Sam scanned the room. "You've done a great job in here. Judging by the size of the crowd, I think you'll be a huge success."

"I hope so. Joe and I have worked so hard."

"Yeah." His gaze toggled between them. "You two make a good team." He lifted his coffee cup in a salute. "I need to get back to work."

"Come back soon." She watched his progress through the shop and out the door before lifting her eyes to Joe's. "Do you think he's okay? He seemed, I don't know, sad or something."

"He's going to be fine."

She cast one more look in the direction of the door. "How's it going? I haven't had a minute to speak to you since we opened."

"Busy. I've discovered I don't have it in me to be a career barista, but I think it's safe to say the beverage side of the bakery is going to be a big moneymaker."

"It may be all we're serving if business doesn't ease up." She frowned at the much-erased chalkboard featuring the available items. "I am down to half a dozen muffins and a single brownie."

"You've still got a couple of whole cakes in the refrigerator, don't you?"

She glanced toward the glass-front cooler. "Yeah?"

"Push comes to shove, you can cut them up and sell them by the slice."

"How had I not thought of that?" She beamed up at him. "You're a genius."

"Isn't that what I've been telling you?" He winked and gave her braid a tug. "Hey, where's my little dude?"

"Mary Jo took him upstairs for lunch and naptime."

He leaned against the counter, arms folded across his chest. "He nearly ran his legs off this morning, table hopping and charming all the guests. By the way, nice marketing move to dress him in a bakery T-shirt. He and Mary Jo worked the room like a couple of pros."

"I don't know what I would have done without her." She sighed as she took up the position beside him. "Today's been a real eye-opener. I planned to man the shop, pour the coffee, replenish the shelves, and watch Jake. Obviously it's unusually busy, but I'm beginning to see this is not a one-person operation."

He'd been telling her the same thing since they first started building, but some things had to be experienced to be understood. "I agree. You're going to need help."

"I don't know the people in town well enough to know who to hire." Worry furrowed her brow while she spoke her thoughts out loud. "And I couldn't afford to pay them very much . . ." She brightened. "I guess I just need to pray about it."

"Man, you sound like Mary Jo."

"Thank you." She flashed a super-charged smile. "That's the nicest compliment you could ever pay me."

She meant it. The most beautiful woman he'd ever seen would prefer to be honored for her faith than be commended for her looks. Truly one in a million.

"And I want *you* to pray with me."

He rolled his eyes. "Exactly like Mary Jo."

The bell over the door chimed, signaling the arrival of another customer. She moved away to greet them. "We'll pray later," she promised over her shoulder.

As it happened, the next prayer he breathed was a solitary one of thanksgiving when the clock finally struck three, and they could lock the front door. Eden had insisted they stay open the entire advertised time, despite the fact they'd run through every crumb an hour ago. Since then, they'd been treating each customer to a free coffee or tea and an invitation to return tomorrow when they had restocked.

A little past three, Eden thanked the few lingering patrons, walking them to the door and waving them out. She flipped the sign in the window from open to closed and after locking the door, sagged against it with a noisy sigh. "What a day."

Joe came out from behind the counter. "You did it."

She shook her head while she approached him. "Not me. *We.* It was a team effort. *We* did it."

When she was not more than two feet away, he opened his arms, and she walked straight into them. "We make a good team."

She nodded against his chest. "The best."

Little feet pattered up. "Hug. Hug." Jake clamped an arm around one of each of their legs.

Joe swept him up into their embrace. "Jake, my man, did you have a good nap?"

"He and I both did." Mary Jo looked from Eden to Joe. "Are we celebrating something?"

"Yes." Eden placed a smacking kiss on her son's cheek. "An amazing first day."

"Oh."

Joe heard the disappointment in the older woman's voice. By the look she sent him, it was clear she expected him to have popped the question, but honestly when did she think he'd had the opportunity?

"Congratulations, dear," Mary Jo said. "Everything was lovely."

"I couldn't have done it without you two. I mean it. I appreciate you both so much. I shudder to think where Jake and I would be if we didn't have you." She leaned over to kiss Mary Jo's cheek, then Joe's, and then Jake's.

"I also shudder to think about opening tomorrow with nothing to sell." She extended her arms to retrieve her son as she nodded toward each of them. "You've earned your freedom. Go home, both of you. Put your feet up and know that I am eternally grateful to you."

"Not so fast." Joe swung Jake out of her reach. "A woman who's worked as hard as you deserves a break. Let's bust out of here for an hour or two and get some fresh air."

"Good idea," Mary Jo said. "Let me take Jake. He can help me make dinner."

Eden shook her head. "I couldn't relax knowing how much I have to do to be ready for tomorrow."

He saw the determination in those blue eyes and knew it was futile to argue. "Okay, we compromise. We bake until five, then we break for an hour or so."

Mary Jo nodded. "Perfect. Be at my house at six thirty for dinner."

Eden frowned. "Are you sure you're up to cooking and seeing us again? You've had a really long day already."

Mary Jo cast a look at Joe before answering. "I wouldn't miss it."

"If you're sure. But Jake stays here." She lifted a palm to silence Mary Jo's protest. "You've babysat enough. Really."

Joe smiled into Mary Jo's concerned eyes. "It's okay." He nodded. "I've got this."

CHAPTER FOURTEEN

After buckling Jake into his car seat, Eden climbed up beside Joe, pulled the seat belt across her lap and clicked it into place. "I'm still not sure this is a good idea."

"Are you kidding? It's a great idea." Joe backed the truck into the street and merged into the sparse afternoon traffic. "All work and no play make Eden burn out."

"Yes, but all play and no work—"

"We worked. I personally just baked four million cookies."

She snorted. "Try four dozen."

"Whatever. And you made at least that many cupcakes—"

"—that need to be iced—"

"You said it yourself. They need to cool." He flashed a smile. "Come on, relax, Florida. Live a little."

She would live a lot better knowing she had a full inventory for tomorrow. No point in arguing when Joe was so obviously determined. She'd just have to finish baking after she put Jake to bed. Good thing she lived over the bakery.

She settled back into the leather seat with a sigh of resignation. "I'll try. So where are we headed?"

"I thought we'd take in some of the lesser sights of Village Green. Now that you've become a resident, you'll want to see what you've committed to." The sudden seriousness in his tone suggested there was more to this excursion than casual sightseeing.

In minutes they'd reached the end of the developed part of town. The paved road narrowed, and open green fields replaced manicured yards. He turned left onto a rutted dirt lane and continued slowly for another quarter mile or so of barbed wire fences, finally rolling to a stop in front of a dilapidated old house.

Eden studied it through the swirl of dust stirred by the truck. With its boarded-up door and windows, sunken roof, rotting porch, and peeling paint, the house was one gust of wind from collapse, not the sort of place usually featured on a highlight reel. She turned to Joe and lifted a brow.

"No tour would be complete without a stop by my old homestead." His expression shuttered when he switched off the engine and climbed out of the truck.

She followed his lead, getting out and retrieving Jake from the back seat. Balancing her son on her hip, she joined Joe in the hot sun on the hard-packed dirt, ten feet from the plywood-covered door.

Silence. Arms folded across his chest, Joe stared at the house. She proceeded cautiously, uncertain as to why he would bring her here. "Interesting place. It looks like it could use some attention. Do you own it?"

He nodded without looking at her. "I've held on to it as a reminder of where I came from." He turned to her. "So what do you think?"

All traces of confident Mr. Tough Guy were gone, revealing a vulnerability that broke her heart. She knew her answer was important, that they were talking about much more than a run-down shack.

She studied the one-story wooden structure, the stark embodiment of hopelessness. "I think that if you've kept it as a trophy, to commemorate all you've overcome and accomplished, then you've accomplished your goal."

She settled Jake on her other hip and faced him. "But if you're using it to remind yourself of your ties to your biological father, then I think it's time to knock it down. Certainly this sad place is a part of your history, but it has no bearing on your future."

Eden reached for his hand, willing him to hear the truth of her words. "You are a wonderful, kind, and generous man, Joseph Wolfe, a truly lovable human being."

Something flared in his eyes while he pressed her fingers. "Do *you* love me?"

She almost laughed. Apparently, it wasn't as obvious as she'd feared. She locked her gaze on his. "Yes, I love you."

His breath whooshed out as though he'd been holding it. "Aww, Eden, I love you too."

He stepped in to take her into his arms, but Jake mistook the gesture and launched himself into the waiting embrace. "Wuv. Wuv."

Joe laughed. "Yes, little man, I love you too."

He shifted Jake to one side to include Eden in the strong circle of his arms. "I love you, both of you. You are the best part of my life, and I want us to be a family." He leaned in, his handsome face inches from hers. "Will you marry me?"

Eden could almost hear romantic music swell in the background, could almost see past the stars in her eyes to brilliant fireworks exploding overhead. This was it, the fairy tale, the moment she'd been afraid to hope for.

A cold wave of reality rushed in, silencing the music and dousing the stars. Eden Lambert didn't deal in fantasy. "That depends."

He straightened, a look of *huh* plastered across his face. "Florida, it's a yes or no question."

She tipped up her chin. "And when you answer my question, I'll give you a yes or no."

Eyes wary, he dipped his chin. "Fair enough. Shoot."

"What about the harem?"

His brow creased. "What harem?"

She tapped her foot. "Your ladies. You know, the names in your little black book."

He held her gaze while he shook his head. "There is no little black book. No harem."

She pulled out of the comfort of his arms to fold hers across her middle and glare up at him. "Sorry if I seem skeptical, but the word on the street says otherwise."

He smiled as though the conversation was funny. "You, of all people, should know how unreliable rumors can be."

She set her fists on her hips. "That's true. I also know that if someone spreads false information about me, I make it my business to correct them."

"And if nobody believes you?"

She opened her mouth to speak, and finding no reply, closed it.

He shifted Jake in his arms. "I dated some in college and afterward. In spite of my background, or maybe because of it, there were plenty of girls willing to go out with me."

"I'll bet."

"I never really connected with anyone. Of course, Matthew and Mary Jo had instilled some pretty high standards for dating, and nowhere in their expectations was there room for anything less than honorable relationships."

"Translated, no fooling around."

He grinned. "Exactly. So after a couple of dates when I realized the relationship had no future, I'd break it off. It became a pattern of serial dating. You'd think with a track record like mine women would avoid me, but they just kept coming around."

He ignored her eye roll.

"Of course, the guys noticed the attention and kidded me about it. Somehow their stories of my exploits kept getting bigger and bigger. I went along with it at first." He kicked at the dirt with the toe of his sneaker. "I guess I thought it was funny that the kid from the wrong side of the tracks, the one who fathers warned their daughters about, never had a shortage of dates. Before I knew it, my reputation had taken on a life of its own. Whenever I tried to set the record straight, they shut me down, like I was being modest." He shrugged. "Eventually, I quit trying."

"I guess having the reputation of Casanova is no hardship for a man."

"Not until I proposed marriage to the woman I love, and she dodged the question."

The woman he loved. That had a nice ring to it. "Not dodging. Fact-finding." She tilted her head. "Do you think Mary Jo believes all the hype?"

"Like the stuff about notching my bedpost?" He chuckled. "No way she believes I'm messing around, or I'd be a dead man. Does she believe that every woman wants me?" His expression softened. "Mary Jo loves me and consequently thinks I'm nearly perfect. I'm sure it never occurred to her that others might not think so too."

"She's right, you know." Eden gazed steadily into his eyes, this man who by the grace of God had overcome staggering odds to become someone she could respect and admire. "You are nearly perfect."

Some of the tension eased from his face. "Does that mean you'll marry me?"

She smiled and nodded. "Yes, I would love to marry you."

Jake nodded as well.

Joe gathered her into his arms and kissed them both, Jake on the nose, Eden on the mouth. "When? I don't think I can wait for one of those year-long engagements. I want to do it right—you deserve the dress and the flowers and the works—but can we do it fast?"

Eden snuggled against his chest. "I bet we could put together a small wedding in a month. I'm sure Mary Jo would help." She pulled back with a start. "Mary Jo! What will she think about us?"

He kissed her again. "She'll say it's about time."

Joe's heart was so filled with joy he could feel the pressure against his rib cage. "This is going to sound cliché, but you've made me the happiest man in the world. You and Jake are a gift, and I want you to know I will love and cherish you both, every day of my life. I've given it a lot of thought, and if you'll let me, I want to adopt Jake. I want him to be my son in every way. And if, down the road, we are blessed with more children, I promise he will be my flesh and bone, just as they are."

Tears sparkled in her eyes. "Yes, I want us to be one family."

He felt a thousand times lighter as he cast a glance over his shoulder at his past. "You ready to ditch this dive and head back to Mary Jo's?"

Eden clasped her hands together. "I can't wait to tell her the news."

After everyone loaded into the truck, he turned it around, kicking up a cloud of dust when he pressed down on the accelerator. An old car turned off the main road onto the drive and proceeded slowly toward them.

Eden looked over at him. "Are you expecting company?"

"No." He squinted through the windshield. "I don't recognize the car."

The gravel lane was too narrow for vehicles to pass comfortably, so Joe steered onto the side and shifted into park. He lowered his window and extended his arm, indicating the other car should stop.

When the vehicles were side by side, the driver braked and slowly rolled down the window, revealing a middle-aged woman with shoulder length brown hair liberally laced with gray.

"Ma'am, you're on private property." His tone was firm but polite. "This road doesn't lead anywhere. You need to turn around up at the house and head back out to the highway."

She lowered her chin. "I'm so sorry."

"Are you lost? If you tell me what you're looking for, I can help you find it."

"No, not lost. Just turned around."

He wrinkled his forehead and continued to stare at her. "Do I know you?"

She ducked her head as if shying from his gaze. "I'm not from around here."

And yet he was almost certain he'd seen her before. "You look familiar to me."

She shook her head slightly and began to roll up her window.

Eden unbuckled her seat belt and leaned across him for better access to the woman. "Wait, what's your name?"

The woman hesitated for so long he didn't think she was going to answer. "Mona."

"As in *Ramona*?"

She nodded.

Eden sat back against her seat with a thump. "Omigosh, Joe," she whispered. "Could that be your mother?"

No way. And yet, he'd seen something. His hammering heart nearly deafened him. "Are you Ramona Wolfe?"

Another slow nod.

Eden found her voice first. "We're headed into town to eat dinner." Her tone sounded normal, as though running across long-lost relatives was an everyday occurrence. "Why don't you join us?"

Ramona shook her head. "Oh no, I couldn't."

"Sure you can," Eden persisted. "There will be plenty of food, and I imagine you and Joe have a lot to catch up on."

"No. I just came by to check." After darting a look at them, she lowered her chin. "I don't want to be in the way."

"You would be very welcome." Careful to keep her action below the line of the window, Eden pinched him hard on the thigh. "It's your mother," she whispered. "Say something."

It took two tries to force the words past his lips. "Please come."

Joe, Eden, and Mary Jo convened around the table in the bakery workroom after they'd tucked Jake into bed upstairs. Joe glanced over at Eden while he measured out the ingredients for scones. Pale shadows appeared below her eyes. "You must be ready to drop."

She had just put a pan of salted caramel fudge brownies in the oven and was spooning lemon icing into a pastry bag to finish off the cupcakes she'd baked earlier. "My body is exhausted, but my mind is spinning. What a day."

Mary Jo beamed. "When the Lord opens the floodgates, He lets it pour. A new business, an engagement, and Joe's mother. All in one day." She clasped her hands over her heart. "So many blessings to be thankful for."

The jury was still out for Joe as to whether they all classified as blessings. The bakery and engagement were clearly the hand of God, but the appearance of his mother after all these years? Honestly, he didn't know how he felt about her.

She seemed nice enough as they'd visited over dinner. True to form, Mary Jo had welcomed her uninvited guest without batting an eye and set an extra place at the table as though Mona were the guest of honor.

She and Eden had done a great job of drawing her into the conversation, asking gentle questions, and warmly encouraging her when she seemed reluctant to speak. He hadn't said much.

Eden looked up from her work to search his face. "How are you, Joe? This is a lot for you to process."

"I'm good. It'll take a while . . ." He wouldn't voice his childish thoughts—that he wasn't about to forgive and forget her abandonment just because she happened to show up.

She laid a comforting hand over his. "Of course it will. You're strangers who just happen to share bloodlines."

He focused on the flour he was pouring into a bowl. "We may never see her again." He kept his tone light. "For all we know, she may have driven away tonight swearing never to return."

Eden shook her head. "She loves you, Joe. Her apologies and remorse for all the lost years seemed genuine."

"She cried enough," Joe said. "She must have gone through an entire box of tissues." If tears equaled authenticity, then she must be the real deal.

"I think she was as surprised as you to actually meet face-to-face" Mary Jo said. "I confess I was shocked to hear her say she's been driving into town at least once a week all this time to catch a glimpse of you."

Not as shocked as he was. Mona told them she'd moved to Fort Worth after his father kicked her out, far enough to escape his abuse but close enough to check on her son. It had taken her a while to get a job and transportation, but once she was able, she'd driven into Village Green regularly, surreptitiously cruising by the house or school to see him.

The idea sounded far-fetched until she provided details she could not have known otherwise, like the red bicycle Matthew and Mary Jo bought him when he was eleven, the second-place ribbon he'd won for cross country as a high school junior that hung on the rearview mirror of his car, or the color of his date's dress for the senior prom.

His mother had been stalking him. She knew about his dorm in college, his first job, his house two blocks away. Creepy to think he'd been completely unaware someone had been watching him, yes, but some part deep inside of him where a bewildered child still dwelt was cheered. Anyone that determined to look in on his progress must have cared about him. Right?

Eden put down the pastry bag. "I don't understand why she didn't try to contact Joe after his father died."

Mary Jo nodded. "I've asked myself the same thing. It's easy to see the poor woman carries a lot of shame for leaving. It's in her posture, demeanor, and speech. She said she doesn't feel worthy to call herself his mother."

Mary Jo slid off her stool to wrap a comforting arm around his waist, leaning her perfumed warmth against his side. "It's early yet, so I won't press you, but I hope one day you'll find it in your heart to forgive her. It wouldn't erase the things she's done or hasn't done, but it would be healing for both of you."

He looked down into the eyes of the woman who'd bandaged his scrapes, cheered his victories, and taught him to pray. "You're the only mother I've ever known."

She raised up on tiptoes to press a kiss to his cheek. "I know, dear one. But I don't mind sharing."

Joe and Sam arrived at Estelle's after the lunch rush. Most of the diners had cleared out by the time Estelle delivered their food.

"So, how's the almost-married man?" Sam stuffed a fry in his mouth.

Joe took a long drink of his sweet tea. "Tired of being engaged."

"What a wimp. How long's it been? A week?"

"Ten days, thank you very much. And it feels like ten years. You have no idea how much stuff goes into planning a *small* wedding."

"No, and unless things pick up around here, I never will."

Joe grinned, thankful for their friendship spanning twenty years. After he'd asked Eden to marry him, he'd gone to Sam the next day to tell him the news personally before the village gossip reached his ears. Their relationship had been a little *off* since the grand opening, and Joe needed to set things right. After a rocky start, they'd talked late into the evening, re-cementing the bond between them. Before he left, Sam agreed to be his best man.

Joe lifted the bun from his hamburger and added extra ketchup. "Consider yourself lucky, my friend. Between the bakery and the wedding prep, the only time I see Eden is over dinner at Mary Jo's when the topic is always flowers or clothes. How many outfits does it take to tie the knot?"

"Beats me." Sam shrugged. "It's a girl thing, I guess. It's nice Mary Jo finally has a daughter to spoil."

"You don't know the half of it." Joe took a bite of his burger. "They've been to every fancy store in Dallas and Fort Worth. From the number of bags and boxes I've seen, they must have cleaned the shops out."

"I'm glad Eden gets the chance to be pampered. I got the impression she didn't have much growing up."

Joe thought about the one dress hanging in her closet. "I think things were pretty tight for her and her mom."

"Is her mother coming to the wedding?"

Joe nodded. "We pick her up at the airport on Thursday night."

"What about your mother?" Sam shook his head. "Man, that feels weird to say. Are you inviting her?"

"I guess so. The ladies want me to." They'd been really understanding about it, expressing how they felt, but leaving it to him to make the final call.

"What about you? Are you okay with her being there?"

He wasn't at first. The abandoned child in him resented that she should be included in this milestone when she hadn't stuck around to raise him. She didn't deserve it.

The adult in him, the one who'd been saved and forgiven by an incredibly gracious God, wanted to rise above petty childishness. He wanted to leave it behind, pressing into the future with Eden and Jake.

He'd been straight with God from the start. He knew he needed to forgive his mother, for both their sakes, but he wasn't feeling it. His head was on board, but his heart wasn't. So his prayer was that God would change his heart.

He'd learned that from Eden. She called it a baby step.

Eden caught her first glimpse of her soon-to-be husband when she topped the wooden stairs of the gazebo in the park. He stood next to Sam and Trey, all three men jaw-droppingly handsome in their dark suits. Joe saw her and winked, stirring the butterflies in her stomach.

Oh, how she loved that man.

At her appearance, the stringed quartet wound up the piece they were playing, the silence alerting the dozen or so guests seated on the platform that the ceremony was about to begin. As the first notes of Pachelbel's Canon in D filled the air, her eighty-year-old matron of honor leaned in to kiss her cheek. "Okay, that's my signal to get going. I love you. I'll see you up front."

"I love you, too, Mary Jo."

Mary Jo moved gracefully down the aisle they'd created through the folding chairs.

It hadn't been easy to convince her she wasn't too old to be her matron of honor, but that was nothing compared to the challenge of finding a dress "befitting a woman of her years." Eden's usually tranquil friend had a deep horror of appearing in tiers of chiffon, like a ruffled cupcake. Finally, just last week, they found a suitable long-sleeved, floor-length dress in Tiffany Blue.

When Mary Jo arrived at the front with Pastor Dale, Joe, Sam, and Trey, the music changed again.

Eden grasped her bouquet, a mix of bright blooms from Mary Jo's garden, in one hand and her son's small hand in the other. They made their way slowly to the front, more out of consideration for his short legs and her long skirt than a need for pomp.

Two-thirds of the way, Jake spotted Joe. Instructions forgotten, he dropped his mother's hand, ran, and leapt into Joe's open arms.

Eden's already full heart expanded with love and gratitude.

Her heavenly Father had blessed her so richly. Joe stepped forward, smiling into her eyes, and he took her hand with his free hand. At his touch, her nerves settled. Her future was safe with this man. They finished the short walk together, stopping in front of a beaming Pastor Dale.

The pastor lifted his Bible and addressed the group. "Dearly beloved . . ."

The photographer worked efficiently, moving down a checklist of requested poses. He snapped dozens of Joe and Eden; more of Joe, Eden, and Jake; then more of him and Eden and the wedding party. The guests waited in their seats, comfortably shaded from the morning sun under the roof of the gazebo, watching the proceedings until everyone was dismissed to Mary Jo's for a luncheon reception.

"That's great," the photographer said. "Just a few more and we're done. Joe and Eden, I need you two, and this time I need the mothers."

Eden's mother popped up from her chair and made her way forward. The photographer saw her approaching and smiled. "Okay, we've got the mother of the bride. Do we have a mother of the groom?"

Joe froze as the unexpected question hung in the air. His beautiful bride met his eyes and winked, a message of solidarity. Whatever he chose to do, she had his back.

The call was his. He could deny his mother and repay a small part of the rejection he'd suffered. Or he could acknowledge her and take one more baby step toward healing.

He didn't know how long he stood there, debating his response. What felt like an eternity was probably no more than a second or two. Finally, he squeezed Eden's hand before releasing it and walking the dozen or so feet that separated him from the woman who'd given him birth.

Her head was bowed, so she hadn't seen his approach. When his feet stopped just in front of hers, she lifted her face, her eyes hopeful, her smile strained.

He extended a hand. "Come on, Mom. Picture time."

Eden shifted Jake's weight, positioning him so his head rested on her shoulder. He'd been having such a wonderful time at the reception, she'd hadn't had the heart to take him upstairs for a nap. When the party wound down, so did he. Minutes ago, when the last guests left, he crashed.

"He looks heavy." Joe reached for Jake. "Why don't you let me take him?"

"Are you sure? I don't want to mess up your suit."

"No worries." He stepped in to make the transfer and paused, his dark eyes searching Eden's face. "Mrs. Wolfe, have I told you how much I love you?"

She smiled up at the man who was the answer to every prayer she hadn't known to pray. "About a million and one times. But I'll never get tired of hearing it, so tell me again."

"I love you, Eden Wolfe." He lifted Jake from her arms and fit the sleeping child to his chest like a pro. "I will love you and this little boy forever."

Seeing her two men together brought a fresh wave of joy and wonder. She lifted a hand to cradle his strong jaw. "Have I mentioned how very much I love you?"

"Not in the last minute or so."

"I love you, Joe Wolfe. You are the very best man I know. And I'm so thankful God brought you into our lives."

Carefully, so as not to crush Jake, Joe leaned in, taking her mouth in a long, tender kiss.

Eden sighed with pleasure. Jesus, Jake, and Joe.

Her own personal paradise.

If you enjoyed this book, will you consider sharing the message with others?

Let us know your thoughts. You can let the author know by visiting or sharing a photo of the cover on our social media pages or leaving a review at a retailer's site. All of it helps us get the message out!

Email: info@ironstreammedia.com

 @ironstreammedia

Iron Stream, Iron Stream Fiction, Iron Stream Kids, Brookstone Publishing Group, and Life Bible Study are imprints of Iron Stream Media, which derives its name from Proverbs 27:17, "As iron sharpens iron, so one person sharpens another." This sharpening describes the process of discipleship, one to another. With this in mind, Iron Stream Media provides a variety of solutions for churches, ministry leaders, and nonprofits ranging from in-depth Bible study curriculum and Christian book publishing to custom publishing and consultative services.

For more information on ISM and its imprints, please visit IronStreamMedia.com